## X marks the corpse

She chose a flat-headed screwdriver first. It fit into the trunk lock, and she jiggled and wiggled it, but nothing happened. Next she chose the smallest of her metal files. It fit into the lock and she pushed it up and to the right until she heard a faint click. The round face of the lock flopped forward and Brenna dropped the file into her toolbox.

The sky was a smoky shade of purple now and she fished in her toolbox for her small flashlight. She turned it on and held the unlit end with her teeth while she grasped each corner of the trunk's lid and slowly lifted it open.

At first, it did look like a bundle of old blankets. No treasure then, she thought. Darn it. But then she noticed the blankets seemed to be wearing an expensive leather belt. She gasped and the flashlight fell out of her mouth and rolled across the grass to plop into the lake.

In seconds its little beam was extinguished, and Brenna was left in the encroaching dark with a trunk that she suspected had a body in it . . .

D0052986

# STUCK ON MURDER

**Lucy Lawrence**

**BERKLEY PRIME CRIME, NEW YORK**

**THE BERKLEY PUBLISHING GROUP**
**Published by the Penguin Group**
**Penguin Group (USA) Inc.**
**375 Hudson Street, New York, New York 10014, USA**

Penguin Group (Canada), 90 Eglinton Avenue East, Suite 700, Toronto, Ontario M4P 2Y3, Canada
(a division of Pearson Penguin Canada Inc.)
Penguin Books Ltd., 80 Strand, London WC2R 0RL, England
Penguin Group Ireland, 25 St. Stephen's Green, Dublin 2, Ireland (a division of Penguin Books Ltd.)
Penguin Group (Australia), 250 Camberwell Road, Camberwell, Victoria 3124, Australia
(a division of Pearson Australia Group Pty. Ltd.)
Penguin Books India Pvt. Ltd., 11 Community Centre, Panchsheel Park, New Delhi—110 017, India
Penguin Group (NZ), 67 Apollo Drive, Rosedale, North Shore 0632, New Zealand
(a division of Pearson New Zealand Ltd.)
Penguin Books (South Africa) (Pty.) Ltd., 24 Sturdee Avenue, Rosebank, Johannesburg 2196,
South Africa

Penguin Books Ltd., Registered Offices: 80 Strand, London WC2R 0RL, England

STUCK ON MURDER

A Berkley Prime Crime Book / published by arrangement with the author

PRINTING HISTORY
Berkley Prime Crime mass-market edition / September 2009

ISBN: 978-0-425-23029-9

BERKLEY® PRIME CRIME
Berkley Prime Crime Books are published by The Berkley Publishing Group,
a division of Penguin Group (USA) Inc.,
375 Hudson Street, New York, New York 10014.
BERKLEY® PRIME CRIME and the PRIME CRIME logo are trademarks of Penguin Group (USA) Inc.

PRINTED IN THE UNITED STATES OF AMERICA

10 9 8 7 6 5 4 3 2 1

*In loving memory of my grandmothers,*
*Adelia Lawrence Norris and Edythe Bell McKinlay.*

# Acknowledgments

When I first started writing, I was too insecure to show anyone my work, but as years went by, and I do mean years, I became more confident and began to reach out to the readers in my life for their input and insights. And so I would like to thank the readers I have come to depend upon for their honesty and kindness. Big "I owe you ones" to Susan McKinlay, Jan Buckwalter, Susie Matazzoni, and Tom Gemberling. There are others, but you four have suffered the most and I thank you for it.

A tip of the brim to agent Jacky Sach for her unflagging belief in my abilities; without you, I'd be floundering in a slush pile somewhere. Another tip of the brim to editor Allison Brandau and to copyeditor Joan Matthews for their brilliance with the details.

Hugs to the divine Ladies of the Loop, my dear writing friends, especially Carolyn Greene, for her unwavering encouragement, support, and lengthy telephone time.

Double hugs for my family, the McKinlays and the Orfs—your absolute faith in me over the years kept me going when there really wasn't any reason to do so.

And lastly, for my dudes: Chris, Beckett, and Wyatt; you three make me laugh every day. You never let me quit and I love you for that.

# Chapter 1

The word *decoupage* is derived from the French *decouper,* which means "to cut out."

"Whatever is she doing?" Ella Porter whispered to her twin sister, Marie.

"Darned if I know," she said.

The elderly women were standing on the sidewalk in front of Vintage Papers, watching Brenna Miller unload a large box from the back of her Jeep.

She was a pretty girl with long, curly auburn hair, which she wore tied at the nape of her neck. Tall and fair, with a dusting of freckles across her nose that made her look younger than she was, Brenna was known for being generous with her smiles. The Porter sisters liked her well enough, but she was not a local. That said it all, in their opinions.

The sisters observed, with their identical eyebrows raised in bewilderment, as Brenna shut the back hatch of her car and pressed her key chain fob until the Jeep gave a rude honk.

Ella started and Marie tsked.

"Is that really necessary?" Marie asked Ella.

"Truly, what does she think will happen here in Morse Point?" Ella agreed. "Why, we've lived here all of our sixty-eight years and we've never locked our car or our house."

"Well, I heard Tenley Morse telling Matt Collins that Brenna's never lived in a small town before," Marie said. "She used to live in Boston. I imagine it's very different there."

Ella shuddered. She didn't even like to leave her own zip code, never mind venture all the way to Boston.

As Brenna walked by, carting the box in her arms, both ladies gave her a big smile as if they hadn't just been talking about her.

Brenna grinned. She knew full well that the Porter twins were gossiping about her. They were known around Morse Point as the keepers of the bodies, as in they knew where they were all buried.

She also knew that the two ladies, as well as the rest of the townspeople, were befuddled by her need to keep her doors locked, both car and house. After all, Morse Point was a small New England town as pretty as a postcard and just as safe.

She adjusted the box on her hip, and her gaze swept over the center of town. The large tree-lined square sported a picturesque white gazebo, which perched in the center of the green like a wedding cake on a reception table. During the summer, the brass band from the Elks Lodge used the pavilion to host free concerts every Saturday night. Residents spread out on blankets under the canopy of maples that dotted the park and listened to butchered renditions of John Philip Sousa's "The Stars and Stripes Forever," played with more heart than you'd find in any city orchestra.

It was like going back in time, Brenna thought, as she glanced down Main Street and saw several shop owners chatting with their customers. There hadn't been a crime worth mentioning in the *Morse Point Courier* in over fifty years, much to the dismay of its editor, Ed Johnson. Brenna knew she should feel completely safe here. But what could she say? You could take the paranoid girl out of the crime-infested city but you couldn't take the paranoia out of the girl. A lifetime of looking over her shoulder was a hard habit to break.

She pulled open the door to Vintage Papers and crab-walked into the shop, trying to manage the door and the big box in her arms without breaking anything.

Sure enough, Tenley already had the worktable set up. It was covered with a bright blue vinyl cloth, and baskets of paper scraps and cutouts had been set out, as well as white glue, paintbrushes, brayers, and damp rags, all ready and waiting for Brenna's decoupage class.

"Hi, Tenley," Brenna said. She set the box down on the floor and arched the kinks out of her back.

"Brenna, you're just in time." Tenley turned from the refreshment table and consulted her watch. "I think we can get a couple of belts of wine in us before the group gets here."

Brenna laughed. "Thank you but no. I don't think my reputation could withstand it. One whiff of wine on me and the Porter twins will cast me as the town drunk."

"Don't worry. They can't. That role is reserved for Bart Thompson," Tenley said. "Every Fourth of July he overin-

dulges and the town police have to tackle him before he
tries to relive his youth and streak across the green like
it's 1972."

Brenna chuckled in surprise. "Doesn't he work at the
hardware store? Tie-dyed T-shirts and long gray ponytail,
right?"

"That's him," Tenley confirmed.

"It must have been so much fun growing up in a town
like this," Brenna said. "Everyone knows everyone."

Tenley narrowed her eyes at her, and Brenna knew her
voice had sounded too wistful. She turned away. She knew
Tenley was thinking about why Brenna had come here,
but she didn't want to talk about what had happened in
Boston. She was getting on with her life and putting her
fears behind her. Mostly.

Brenna and Tenley Morse had remained good friends
since their years together at Boston University. When Tenley heard her former roommate was looking to leave the
city, she had offered her a clerking position at Vintage
Papers.

Brenna had accepted the offer and never looked back.
She had transitioned easily from working at an art gallery
in Boston to selling specialty papers in Morse Point.

Knowing how much Brenna loved to decoupage, Tenley let her sell some of her creations in the shop and had
her teaching decoupage classes in the evening. They had
developed quite a devoted little group over the past few
months, although Brenna suspected it was gossip the ladies came for more than the art of decoupage. No matter.
She was getting paid to do something she loved. Life
didn't get much better than that.

She opened her box and began placing plain white

birdhouses at each seat. They had eight ladies signed up for the ongoing class, and every week they tried to tackle a new project.

"Birdhouses?"

Brenna turned to see Cynthia Ripley, the mayor's wife, and her best friend, Phyllis Portsmyth, enter the store. Given Cynthia's condescending tone, she wondered if she should have accepted Tenley's offer of a glass of wine.

"Why, hello, Cynthia, Phyllis," Brenna greeted the two ladies.

They were the picture of middle-aged chic: rail thin with bobbed blond hair that was stacked in the back, and wearing a diamond at every pulse point. Phyllis was known for the five-carat yellow Portsmyth sparkler she wore on her right ring finger, while Cynthia favored a four-carat pink diamond pendant.

In color-coordinated Ann Taylor outfits, the only difference Brenna could spot between them was that Phyllis had an air of entitlement—she came from old money and had married old money—which Cynthia lacked.

According to the Porter sisters, Cynthia had clawed her way out of a hard life in Dorchester and up the social ladder by marrying Jim Ripley, whom she then pushed into politics. Once Jim was elected, Cynthia had attached herself to Phyllis and slowly metamorphosed into an imitation of her new friend, with the same clothes, hairdo, and patronizing tone. But no matter how much Joy perfume Cynthia spritzed on, she would never be able to cover up the smell of desperation that surrounded her. It was their one true difference, to Brenna's eye. Well, that and Phyllis had bigger boobs. More money will do that for a girl.

"Honestly, birdhouses?" Cynthia said again.

"Yes, don't you think that's a bit pedestrian?" Phyllis asked. The two women looked at Brenna with matching expressions of disdain.

Looking past them, she could see the rest of the ladies, including the Porter twins, file into the shop, watching the exchange with avid interest.

"Perhaps," Brenna said.

Tenley was making gagging motions behind Phyllis's back, and Brenna quickly looked away so she wouldn't laugh. There was no love lost between Tenley Morse and Phyllis Portsmyth, as their families had vied for the position of most powerful family in Morse Point for generations.

Brenna had one more birdhouse in the box that was her own creation. She had made it to give the class an idea of what theirs could look like when they were finished. She lifted it out of the box and released it from its bubble wrap cocoon. She heard someone gasp and felt herself flush with pleasure. It had come out extraordinarily well, if she did say so herself.

She placed the birdhouse in the center of the large worktable and stood back to watch the ladies crowd around it. She had used many of Tenley's collectible papers as well as a few from her own personal reserve. Around the house fluttered colorful cutout butterflies in various sizes while the roof had been decorated with layers of old seed packets that featured pen and ink drawings of flowers.

"That is just charming," Ella Porter declared.

"More than charming," Marie corrected her. "It is outstanding."

Ella gave her a dark look. The elderly twins were known to be a tad competitive, even when it came to doling out praise.

"It is said," Brenna stated, loudly enough so that the entire room could hear her, "that Marie Antoinette and her Court favored flowers and butterflies for their birdhouses, but if you think that's too pedestrian, I'm sure we can come up with something else."

Phyllis let out a sniff and said, "Obviously, you misunderstood me."

Cynthia Ripley gave a similar sniff and followed her friend to the refreshment table for a glass of wine.

"That's telling 'em," Tenley whispered in her ear as she moved to stand beside her. "So, did Marie Antoinette really decorate birdhouses?"

"I don't know if she did birdhouses exactly, but she was a known decouper," Brenna whispered back. "She and her friends were quite passionate about it."

Tenley leaned back and grinned at her. "You are just a perfect fit here, aren't you?"

Brenna glanced around Tenley's shop. It was a full sensory experience. Racks of handmade papers lined one wall in an explosion of color, books of paper samples were stacked on another table, and the rest of the room was stocked with shelves of glue, paint, markers, and scissors. She loved the woodsy smell of the handmade papers as well as the feel of them, from the satiny finishes to the chunky matte sheets with flowers embedded in them. Her fingers positively itched to create something clever. Vintage Papers was one of her favorite places to be.

"I belong in the shop," she agreed. "It's the rest of Morse Point I'm not so sure about."

"Don't worry." Tenley patted her arm. "A few more months here and we'll rinse that city stink off of you."

Brenna gave her an alarmed look and Tenley laughed at her as she made her way back to the refreshment table.

Tenley had been born and raised in Morse Point. In fact, the town was named for Tenley's family. With her long blond hair and friendly, wide smile, Tenley was liked by everyone in town. Well, everyone except Phyllis Portsmyth and her two girls. They resented the ease with which Tenley was embraced as the town's favorite daughter.

But truly, why wouldn't she be? Tenley had been the homecoming queen, class president, and a varsity tennis player. She spent weekends bringing meals and her sunny disposition to the homebound elderly, and she volunteered at the local home for troubled youth. She really was an amazing person, and Brenna was grateful to be her friend. Tenley had given her a place to run to when she needed to get away, and Brenna was glad that she could contribute something to Tenley's store to help make it a success.

She waited while her class fortified themselves with crackers, Brie, and bubbling glasses of Riesling. Once all of her students were settled in their seats, she circled the table to watch as they selected their materials from the papers and cuttings that Tenley had laid out.

A couple of the women chose the ivy garland and set to work cutting out the intricate pattern, while others chose the lilacs and bluebirds. The room became hushed as the women snipped at their chosen patterns.

"Let go!" Ella Porter snapped at her twin.

"I will not," Marie balked. "I had it first."

"Did not."

"Did too."

"Here we go again," Brenna whispered to Tenley. "Are they too big to be put in time-out?"

Tenley managed to turn her snort into a cough, while Brenna hustled over to the twins.

"Ladies, I am sure we have another sunflower in the

back. Let me just borrow this one to match it," Brenna said.

She tried to take the sunflower, but neither one would let go. She gave a gentle tug, but they both tightened their grip, and Brenna wondered if she would have to pry their fingers off one at a time.

The bells hanging on the front door gave a terse jangle, and everyone turned to see who had yanked open the door. Brenna used the moment to snatch the sunflower out of the ladies' hands. They both gave her a put-out look, but she just smiled and turned to the door.

Jim Ripley, the town mayor, entered the shop. His clothes were rumpled and his comb-over had flopped onto to the wrong side of his head, making him look like a lopsided rooster. He was also red from his forehead to his jowls, adding to his gallinaceous appearance. He scanned the room, passing over all of the women until he saw Brenna.

"It's imperative that I speak with you," he said.

# Chapter 2

Many of the best examples of decoupage come from Venice, Italy, where cabinetmakers began the style of mixing paintings with furniture in the late-seventeenth century.

Brenna stared at the mayor. Aware that the entire room was watching her, she forced a smile. She did not want to give the Porter twins even more to gossip about.

"Ahem." Cynthia Ripley cleared her throat.

The mayor cast her a cursory glance, barely removing his eyes from Brenna, who had no idea what to say. He sidled over to the table, still watching Brenna, as he leaned over and kissed the side of Phyllis's cheek with gusto.

"Jim!" Cynthia snapped while Phyllis blushed to the roots of her bottle blond hair.

"What? Oh!" Mayor Ripley looked away from Brenna and saw his wife glowering at him while her friend flushed with embarrassment. His practiced politician's smile lost some of its luster. "Oh, I am so sorry, my dear. Pardon me, Phyllis. I thought you were . . . oh, dear."

"Really, Jim, I should think you'd know your own wife," Cynthia snapped.

He looked like a chastened schoolboy as he leaned forward to peck Cynthia's rigid cheek. "Of course, dearest, so sorry. Again, Phyllis, forgive me. I have some business to discuss with Ms. Miller, and then I'll be on my way."

"Of course," Brenna said, feeling bad for him. Honestly, she wasn't sure *she'd* be able to tell the difference between the two women from behind. "Shall we step outside?"

"Excellent," Mayor Ripley said. His polished public grin was back in place and at full wattage. "After you."

Brenna led the way out into the cool April evening. There was a dampness to the air that promised rain overnight. The old-fashioned streetlamps that surrounded the square cast large pools of golden light, and she could see moths dancing in and out of their glow.

She glanced through the window of Vintage Papers and saw Tenley trying to get the class back on task, but the ladies had all stopped what they were doing to watch Brenna and Mayor Ripley.

He followed her gaze and said, "Perhaps we should walk."

Brenna fell into step beside him. Mayor Ripley was a stocky man, who came up only to her ear, so she shortened her stride to match his. He wore a white dress shirt with the cuffs rolled back to his elbows and a pair of navy blue suspenders, which kept his creased dress slacks hovering just below the pronounced bulge of his belly. His tie was loose, the knot hanging beneath the open neck of his shirt. She got the feeling he was agitated about something, but she couldn't for the life of her figure out what it had to do with her.

"I'm going to get right to the point," he said. "How well do you know your landlord, Nate Williams?"

Okay, she hadn't seen that one coming. Her face must have shown her surprise as Mayor Ripley continued hurriedly, "You've lived in one of his cabins on the lake for how long now?"

"A little over a year."

"Ed Johnson told me that you and Nate Williams are friends," he said. He studied her out of the corner of his eye, and Brenna knew he was looking for confirmation of this information. Well, he wasn't going to get it.

"Why would you be talking to Ed Johnson about Nate Williams and me?" she asked. She tried to keep the irritation out of her tone, but it was difficult. Somehow, when the Porter sisters talked about her, it was amusing, but when it was the mayor and the editor of the local newspaper, she felt violated.

"Nate Williams has been buying up property around Morse Point Lake for the past few years," he said. "This is property that could be used for greater benefit for the town."

"Like building a park?" she asked, trying to understand.

"Yes, like a park," the mayor said. He nodded with enthusiasm. They reached the corner of the street and turned back toward the shop, when he added, "Only privately owned."

"I don't understand," she said. "How can a privately owned park benefit the town?"

"Revenue, my dear, it all comes down to revenue," he said.

"I'm not sure I'm following," she said, although she was starting to get a sinking feeling in the pit of her stomach.

"If Williams sells some of the lots he's bought around

the lake to the town, then we can sell them to a developer, who can put in vacation town houses," he said. "The tax revenue alone would give the town a real shot in the arm, not to mention an increased customer base for local businesses like your friend Miss Tenley's paper shop."

"And you're talking to me about this because . . . ?" She let the question dangle.

"Ed says you know Williams better than anyone. In fact, he says you're the only person he talks to in all of Morse Point."

Brenna shook her head. If she was considered the expert on Nate Williams, then they were really reaching. Nate was a man of mystery as far as she was concerned. Their "friendship" was based upon their mutual love of baseball and his sweet tooth.

Shortly after she had moved into her cabin, she had begun bringing Nate tins of brownies, cookies, or what have you whenever her weekly baking urge hit. It was her way of repaying him for the ludicrously low rent he charged her.

What she did know about Nate, she had learned from her time working in a gallery in Boston. There had been a tremendous buzz about him in the art world ten years prior. His large canvases had used abstract lines of colors reminiscent of the Color Field paintings of the early 1960s. He was considered the next genius, but then he had abruptly dropped out of the New York art scene and gone into seclusion. No one knew why.

Nate didn't say as much, and she knew better than to ask, but she suspected he moved here to leave that world behind him. In the year she had known him, she'd never seen him pick up a brush or heard him talk about his former life.

Figuring she'd better head the mayor off at the pass, she said, "He's my landlord, and that's as far as it goes."

"Still, you can't deny he talks to you," Mayor Ripley insisted.

"Well, no, but I hardly think a dialogue on the Yankees versus the Red Sox is an opening to tell him that he should sell some of his property to the town."

"But of course it is," he said. He patted her shoulder as they stopped in front of Vintage Papers. "He'll listen to you. I'm sure of it."

"Why would he listen to me?"

"You're his tenant. He'll value your opinion."

To her credit, Brenna didn't laugh out loud.

"But what if I don't want a bunch of vacation town houses in my backyard?" she asked.

"You need to think of the greater good," the mayor said in what sounded like an overly rehearsed campaign speech. "How long do you think your friend can stay in business in a specialty shop without a broader client base?"

Brenna opened her mouth to protest, but the mayor spoke over her. "Now, here's what you need to tell him. He should consider selling half of his property around the lake to the town, at market value, of course. Then if he would consent to spearheading the campaign to bring tourists and new homeowners to Morse Point, why, that would be the cherry on top. He's our biggest celebrity, after all; he could bring them in by the busload."

"Spearhead the campaign?" Brenna repeated dully. "Have you discussed this with Nate?"

Mayor Ripley gave her a pained look, and Brenna gathered that he had and it had not gone well.

"You can do this," the mayor insisted. "It's quite simple; just tell him what I told you. Now, I'll be back tomorrow to hear about your progress."

"Tomorrow?" Brenna repeated. "But I haven't—"

"Time is money," he said, interrupting her again. "Speaking of which, your class is waiting for you."

Brenna looked through the window and saw her class still watching them. The Porter sisters were craning their necks, each trying to be taller than the other without actually rising out of her seat, while Cynthia Ripley was glaring at her. Lovely.

When she turned back, Mayor Ripley was gone, leaving her feeling as flattened as a decoupage cutout under a brayer.

Brenna spent the rest of the class distracted and under the scrutinizing eye of Cynthia Ripley. She hoped Mayor Ripley had told his wife why he wanted to talk to her; otherwise she could only imagine what Cynthia must be thinking. Judging by her scowl, the mayor had not enlightened her.

The Porter sisters had tried to find out what the mayor wanted, but Brenna dodged their queries by giving a long-winded monologue on how important it was to use a sharp pair of cutting scissors. She showed them how to check that the points matched up, and by the time she'd finished her cutting demonstration, most of the class wore glazed expressions and seemed quite happy to call it a night.

"I can't believe he asked you to do that." Tenley was indignant on her behalf.

Brenna shrugged. She put the half-finished birdhouses on a shelf to dry while Tenley packed up the scissors, brayers, and glue.

"What are you going to do?" Tenley asked.

"I don't know," she said. "You know the mayor better than I do. How annoying will he be if I don't do this?"

Tenley rolled her eyes.

"That bad?" Brenna asked.

She nodded. "Let's put it this way: He was elected mayor because he literally went door to door and badgered everyone to vote for him. Frankly, we elected him to shut him up."

"Wonderful. So, I have to choose between alienating the mayor or my landlord." She gathered up the paper cutouts and stored them in a box for the next class.

"Looks like it," Tenley agreed.

"Well, there's only one way to settle it," Brenna said. She fished a coin out of her jean pocket and said, "Heads, I talk to Nate. Tails, I blow off the mayor."

"The coin toss!" Tenley laughed. "I haven't thought of that in years. We used to use that to decide whether to date someone or not."

"It worked then," Brenna pointed out. "Remember that cute frat boy who asked you out and you couldn't decide? The coin said tails and you said no, and then we found out he had a pregnant girlfriend."

"Oh yeah, what a creep," Tenley said with a shudder. "And when you flipped it, it said heads and you dated James for four years." Brenna made a face and Tenley said, "Oh, bad example. Sorry."

Brenna put the quarter on her thumb and flipped it. It landed on the table with a thunk and a spin and finally wobbled onto its side.

Tenley leaned over it. "Heads. Looks like you have a date."

# Chapter 3

Late in his life, modern artist Henri Matisse made paper cuttings an integral part of his work.

Brenna had not done any baking since she'd felt the need for a batch of butterscotch squares, which had sorely depleted her flour supply. She scrounged the cupboards in her kitchenette for a quick idea but could only come up with teddy bear–shaped graham crackers, several squares of bittersweet chocolate, and a bag of mini-marshmallows. The bribe-ability factor of a s'mores casserole was questionable, but she was going to have to give it a go. She greased a small glass dish, made layers, like a lasagna, of teddy bears, marshmallows, and chopped-up chocolate. Then she broiled it until the marshmallows on top turned golden brown.

She glanced through the window by her front door, and saw that Nate's lights were still on. His was the largest cabin and it sat directly across the inlet from hers. It was only eight thirty, so she figured it wasn't too late to go visit him.

She set the dish on her porch railing while she locked her front door. Then, using her red-checked potholder mittens, she carried the dish with both hands as she followed the well-worn path along the water's edge.

She took in the signs of early spring. Crickets and tree frogs sang their nightly symphony, and the chilly evening air made a fine mist rise from the hot dish in her hands.

She climbed the three steps to Nate's porch and knocked on the front door with the toe of her shoe. Instantly, there was an explosion of canine proportions on the other side of the door as Hank, Nate's golden retriever, went into a frenzy of barking.

Brenna moved to stand in front of the window, so that Hank would see her and settle down, but she was distracted by her own disheveled reflection and frowned. Her hair had come out of the band at the nape of her neck and was now hanging in her face, making her look as if she'd spent a hard day scrubbing toilets. Fabulous.

Why hadn't she thought to run a comb through her hair or put on some lipstick? Darn it. Not that it mattered, she reminded herself, they were just landlord and tenant. Still, it would have boosted her confidence, given that she was about to become a huge buttinsky.

Nate opened the door with one hand on Hank's collar to keep the dog from launching himself at Brenna. He, too, was dressed casually in jeans and sneakers and a long-sleeved T-shirt. His brown wavy hair was messy, as if he'd recently run his fingers through it, and there was a shadow of stubble on his chin as if he had opted not to shave that morning.

"My dentist is going to love you," he said. His mouth tipped up to one side and she knew he was teasing her.

"Maybe I'll have him put me on retainer," she said.

"You keep this up and he's going to put me *in* retainers," he retorted.

"You're right," she said. She glanced at the dish in her hands and back at him and schooled her features into one of grave concern. "I really shouldn't unload this s'mores casserole on you. Maybe I have some broccoli that I could steam and bring that over instead."

"Hey, I never said I minded if my dentist loves you." Nate let go of Hank and reached to take the dish from her.

"It's hot," she warned and held it away from him. Hank took the opportunity to jump up, and she turned so his paws landed on her hip while he gave her a sloppy kiss on the cheek.

"Down, Hank," Nate ordered. Hank ignored him and Brenna laughed as Nate had to grab his collar again and pull him down. "Come on in."

Brenna followed him into the house as he led the way through the living room and into the kitchen.

Nate's cottage was exactly like hers but had one more bedroom. Outside they were the same white clapboard with green shudders and a small front porch, and inside they had the same hardwood floors and white plaster walls. But where Brenna had hung prints of her favorite masterpieces on her walls, Nate kept his bare. She often wondered about that but figured it would be rude to ask.

He led her through the living room, which hosted a large-screen TV and several cushy leather chairs, and into the kitchen. She noticed the TV was off.

"Catch the game tonight?" she asked.

"The Red Sox got lucky," he replied.

"Lucky? Ha! They spanked your precious Yankees," she said. "What was the final score? I can't recall."

"Tentothree," he mumbled.

"I'm sorry," she said. "I didn't catch that."

He looked chagrined. "Ten to three, as you know full well."

"Yes, but I just love to hear it coming from a Yankee fan's lips," she said.

He squinted at her. "There will be payback."

"Maybe," she said, but her voice was doubtful.

She placed the casserole dish on a round cast-iron trivet on the cobalt blue tile counter, while Nate let Hank out the back door and then fetched two plates, two forks, and a large serving spoon.

"S'mores casserole, eh?" he asked. He leaned close over the dish and inhaled. "Smells awesome."

"I just threw it together," she said with a shrug. He had no idea how true that was, and she didn't plan to enlighten him.

She studied him as he dug the big spoon into the dish. With his wavy hair hanging over his brow just so and his rugged features, he was unquestionably a handsome man. But it was his watchfulness that always caught her off guard. He had a way of looking at her, of giving her his full attention, which made her feel as if she were the most important person in the world. She could absolutely see why the art world had gone gonzo for him. He was a genius and a hottie, a lethal combination, for sure.

Nate pushed a plate in front of her. Her casserole appeared to be a gooey mess, but that seemed right, given the sticky situation she found herself in. How was she going to tell Nate what the mayor said? Should she just lob it out there and hope he responded well? Or should she lead up to it slowly, and hope he caught on?

She watched as he spooned a bite of the decadent casserole into his mouth.

"Mayor Ripley thinks you should sell half of your property around the lake to the town so they can develop it for tourism and he wants you to spearhead the campaign." It all came out in a rush and some of the words blurred together, but judging by his bug-eyed expression, Nate got the gist.

He opened his mouth to speak and promptly began to choke. Brenna looked at him in alarm as he began to cough and splutter. She reached around and thumped him on the back. Hard.

He held up a hand and nodded that he was okay but still he hacked. She grabbed a glass from the cupboard and filled it with water from the tap. He took a long sip and then shook his head.

"You want to run that by me when I don't have my mouth full?" he asked.

"Sorry," she said. She gave him an apologetic look. "I didn't mean to spew it out like that. Mayor Ripley stopped by my decoupage class tonight. Apparently, Ed Johnson told him that you and I are friends." She found it difficult to meet his gaze at this point and turned her attention to twirling her fork in the dessert on her plate.

"And?" he prompted her. She glanced quickly at his face, but his features were set and she couldn't fathom what he was thinking. Still, she felt oddly pleased that he didn't balk at the term *friends*.

"Oh, and so Mayor Ripley thought I should be the one to tell you to sell your property and star in the campaign to court tourists."

"Hmm. And what do you think I should do?" he asked her.

His gray eyes were intent upon her face, and Brenna was again hit with the sensation that she had captured his complete attention. It was flattering and a bit unnerving.

"That's really up to you, isn't it?" she asked.

"Yes, but I want to know what you think," he said.

She looked over her shoulder through the living room window toward the lake and said, "I like it the way it is."

He gave her a warm smile. They ate silently for a few moments, the steady tick-tock of the kitchen clock the only sound in the small house.

"When does Dim Dipley expect you to report back to him?" he asked.

"Dim Dipley?" she repeated.

"My little pet name for the mayor," he said.

Brenna laughed and he grinned in return.

"He said he would check up on my progress tomorrow. He's a bit tenacious," she said.

"A bit." Nate was staring out the back window toward the woods beyond. She followed his gaze but could see nothing in the darkness.

"Well, you can tell Dim for me that I will spearhead a campaign," he said. "In fact, he can be sure to see a piece about it in the *Courier* the day after tomorrow."

"You will?" Brenna asked. She was shocked. She had been so sure he would be furious with the mayor.

"Yep," he said. He scraped his fork against his plate to get the last of the melted chocolate, and he looked at her with a mischievous sparkle in his eye. "Seconds?"

He looked entirely too happy, and she knew it wasn't just a chocolate buzz from her casserole. No, she had the distinct feeling that he was up to something, but given his private nature, she was hesitant to ask. She'd just have to wait and see what this man of mystery had up his sleeve.

She didn't have long to wait. Mayor Ripley found her at Vintage Papers the next day, and she told him exactly what Nate had said. He clapped his hands, looking delighted, and credited her with Nate's cooperation.

Brenna was left feeling ill at ease. She had no doubt that it was due to the calculating gleam in Nate's eyes when he had said good night to her. She wondered if she should warn the mayor, but she was still a little peeved with him for putting her in the middle of this.

It was not a tremendous surprise to Brenna when, a few days later, the *Morse Point Courier* ran the story of Nate's campaign to save Morse Point Lake from the evil clutches of Mayor Dim Dipley. And yes, that was how they printed his name.

The clincher, however, was the line drawing penned by Nate that accompanied the article, in which Mayor Ripley was depicted, with his comb-over and suspenders, as a large, sweaty giant handing over the town of Morse Point to a black-cloaked grim reaper with the words *land developer* on its scythe in exchange for a bucket overflowing with cash.

"Oh, my," Tenley breathed as she scanned the newspaper Brenna had slapped down in front of her moments before.

Tenley was sitting at the bar in the Fife and Drum, Morse Point's oldest restaurant, which looked out over the town green. It was their Friday night ritual to close the shop early and treat themselves to a glass of wine in the bar and a couple of chicken Caesar salads in the restaurant.

Tenley had been talking with Matt Collins, the bartender, when Brenna arrived with the paper. As Tenley finished reading and turned to stare at her, Matt pulled the paper close and gave a low whistle when he took in the picture of the mayor.

"Heads are going to roll," he said. He glanced up at them and then squinted over their shoulders through the picture window. "Right about now, by the look of things."

Tenley and Brenna turned to look out the window as well. Brenna gasped. Standing on the steps of the town hall, which was adjacent to the restaurant, were Nate Williams and Mayor Ripley. Judging by their irate expressions and wild arm gestures, they were not exchanging pleasantries about the weather.

Brenna rushed through the front door. She couldn't help feeling as if this was her fault. She should never have told Nate what the mayor wanted. She should have just put Ripley off until he gave up the whole idea. Realistically, he would have approached Nate himself and they'd be in exactly this same spot, but at least she would not feel like part of it was her fault.

"Look, Dim Dipley," Nate was yelling. "I am not now nor am I ever going to sell off my property so that you can line your fat pockets with more money."

"That's slander!" Mayor Ripley shouted back, waving a chubby finger at Nate. "I could sue you for that."

"Really?" Nate asked. "Are you telling me you're not planning to profit from this?"

"This is for the good of the town," Ripley protested. "I am ensuring economic stability for future generations."

"Pah!" Nate scoffed. "The only economics you're interested in are the balances of your own bank accounts."

"That's it!" Mayor Ripley balled up his chubby fists. "I

am going to sue you for libel and you'll have to sell your property just to cover your legal expenses."

"Go ahead," Nate dared him. "But I'll sell my property over my dead body. Or better yet, over *your* dead body!"

With that, he turned and stormed down the steps of the town hall, climbed into his ancient Ford pickup truck, and drove off. The mayor turned on his heel and stomped back up the steps into the town hall, slamming the large door behind him.

People all around the square had stopped what they were doing to watch, and now a buzz of conversation hummed on the air like a busy swarm of bees.

# Chapter 4

Traditionally, wooden objects are used for decoupage, especially furniture, but almost any surface can be used, even glass and soap.

The feud between Nate and the mayor was the talk of the town. Ed Johnson, the *Morse Point Courier*'s editor-in-chief, was found in Stan's Diner having raptures that his newspaper had run the first piece of art produced by Nate Williams in years. The newspaper had actually had to run extra copies to meet the demand, and rumor had it the story might get picked up on the wire. Ed was ecstatic.

In his late fifties, Ed had waited his entire professional career for his Pulitzer moment. It was easy to see, as he chain-smoked and slugged back coffee with ill-concealed glee, that he thought this was it. He had all of the coffee-house regulars enthralled with his tall tale of how he had wrestled the story and the drawing out of Nate Williams. As he paced between their booths, with his big bald head perched on his stringy neck and his beak-like nose twitching, Brenna couldn't help but notice Ed's resemblance to a plucked chicken. When he saw her standing at the counter, he stopped short. Uh-oh.

Brenna glanced back over the counter at Stan, whose big, sausage-shaped fingers were putting the froth on her café latte. Stan took his froth very seriously, and it would do no good for her to tell him to hurry it up.

"Well, if it isn't Morse Point's loveliest new resident," Ed said as he took the empty seat beside her at the counter. "How are you, Ms. Miller?"

Brenna sighed when she saw Stan trying to sculpt her froth into a swan shape. There would be no quick escape. She was just going to have to deal with Ed head on.

She turned to face him. "I'm fine. How are you, Mr. Johnson?"

"Please call me Ed," he said. He smiled what she was sure he considered to be his most engaging smile, but it just made her feel greasy, like she'd been dropped into Stan's fryer.

"And how is our mutual friend Nate Williams?" he asked.

"As far as I know, my landlord is fine," she said.

"Really?" he asked. "No fallout from the mayor then?"

"I suppose you'd have to ask him," she said. "Since you're such close friends."

He pursed his lips, momentarily thwarted. Brenna took this as confirmation that Nate had gone back to his reclusive ways and was no longer communicating with the editor-in-chief.

Stan placed her latte in front of her with a flourish, and Brenna had to admit that she was impressed. The swan was dusted lightly with cinnamon and bobbed gently on the surface of the coffee as if ready to swim away.

"It's beautiful, Stan," she said. "Thank you."

Stan did not smile—he never smiled—but he flexed his forearm, which showed off his Navy tattoo, and he nodded at her.

She paid for the coffee, adding a healthy tip for sheer aesthetic value. Ed opened his mouth to speak, but she cut him off with a cheery, "Bye, fellas, have a great day."

She spent the rest of the day working the counter at Vintage Papers. Tenley had just received an order of Bertini Italian print paper, and Brenna was sorting the sheets and pricing them before putting them out. In addition to the big money makers of greeting cards and wedding invitations, Tenley prided herself on carrying an assortment of specialty papers from around the world. It was one of the things Brenna loved best about the shop.

The Porter sisters popped in later that morning, seemingly to examine the new papers, but Brenna knew it was really to see if she had any more information about Nate's scuffle with the mayor. She was happy to report that she did not.

"I heard from Mimi Gardener, she works in the town tax assessor's office, that Mayor Ripley was going to hire the law firm, Payne and Zuffren, to represent him in a slander suit against Nate Williams," Ella said. She fingered the Bertini paper called "scrolls" as she spoke. Brenna watched her pink fingertip trace the swirling patterns of color.

She pressed her lips together. If she said nothing, then the conversation would have to die, even if it was a slow and painful death.

"Well, I heard from Jeanette Milton, she's the organist at the church, that Nate Williams was going to countersue for harassment," Marie said. "Has he said as much to you, Brenna?"

"No," she said.

The twins gave her identical vexed looks when she didn't elaborate.

"You know, you really should tell him not to," Marie said. "Lawsuits never solve anything. You're his friend. Tell him to make up with the mayor. I'm sure he'd listen to you."

"I am not his friend," Brenna protested. "I'm just his tenant."

So what if she and Nate shared a love of baked goods and baseball? That hardly made her his friend or put her in a position to tell him what to do about the mayor. And thinking of Mayor Ripley, Brenna decided this whole mess was his fault. If he hadn't asked her to speak to Nate, the two men wouldn't be feuding now. Well, maybe they would, but she wouldn't have any part in it.

As far as Brenna was concerned, she had learned her first real lesson about small town life. She was never again going to get involved in something that was none of her business.

That resolution lasted for several days. Brenna ignored the emergency town council meeting that the mayor called. Because Nate had yet to rent out half of his ten cabins, the mayor was proposing to have the cabins ruled a blight on the community, to be confiscated by the town using eminent domain. Although she feared she might lose her home, Brenna avoided the meeting and stayed out of the debate.

Thankfully, Silas Cooper gave an eloquent speech to the town council about a man's right to own his own property without fear of it being seized by the government just because it wasn't up to snuff. Silas's farm had a reputation for being a tad sloppy, but his family had farmed in Morse

Point for six generations. The council voted down the mayor's proposal four to one. After that, Brenna had been sure the worst of it had passed, but no.

Nate applied for the cabins to be registered as historic properties. They had been built in the early 1900s as vacation getaways for rich Bostonians looking to escape to the country. That was in the flush times before the Great Depression. Roger Chisholm, the president of the local historical society, was delighted by Nate's request. The mayor was not. If the cabins achieved a historic designation, there would no chance of tearing them down to develop the land.

The mayor then decided to go for Nate's wallet, and Brenna woke up one morning to find the tax assessor for the town standing on her front porch, measuring her cabin. It was an obvious ploy on Mayor Ripley's part to increase the property value on the cabins and drive Nate out.

Still, Brenna stayed out of it. She was absolutely, positively not going to get involved. Period. End of discussion.

She stayed her course, refusing to get sucked into the drama, right up until a week later when Matt Collins made an unexpected appearance in the shop.

Brenna was sitting at the large worktable in the back, soaking cutouts of apples in a bowl of water. Once saturated with water, the apples would be coated with glue and pasted onto an old ceramic jug. She was making it as an example for a future class project.

The bells jangled when Matt pulled open the front door and stepped inside. With his brawny build and masculine good looks, he seemed as out of place as a Great Dane in a litter of toy poodles.

Brenna saw Tenley start and watched her face turn just the faintest shade of pink. Even if she hadn't looked, Brenna would have known it was Matt Collins who had just come into the shop. Tenley always looked as if she'd just been plugged into a wall socket whenever Matt was around.

"Hi, Matt," Tenley greeted him from where she was arranging the Bertini paper into a striking display.

"Hi, Tenley," he said in return. His gaze swept over the shop in appreciation. "Nice place you've got here."

"Thanks," she said.

Brenna wasn't positive, but she thought Tenley's face might have gotten even pinker. She'd been watching these two do-si-do around one another for over a year now. She couldn't help but hope that Matt had finally screwed up the nerve to ask Tenley out.

"Is there something I can help you find?" Tenley asked.

"Oh, no thanks," he said. He ran a hand through his thick thatch of blond hair as if he, too, was feeling a bit awkward. "I found her."

He turned to face Brenna. Out of the corner of her eye, she was sure she saw Tenley stiffen, but when she glanced at her, Tenley gave her a small smile, although it didn't quite reach her eyes.

"What can I do for you, Matt?" Brenna asked. She had no idea what to expect. She'd never gotten anything other than a friendship vibe from him, so she knew he wasn't here to ask her out. Maybe he had a decoupage project for her. That would be nice.

"Well," he hesitated. "It's not really any of my business, but . . ."

"But?" she encouraged him.

"Have you been out to your place at all today?"

"Not since I left this morning," she said. "Why? Is something wrong?"

Matt cupped the back of his neck with his right hand and said, "Not if you mean something like a flood or a fire."

"Matt, spill it," Brenna said. She pulled the paper apples out of the water, letting them drip dry for a few seconds. She laid them out on a towel and was half out of her seat in anticipation of a calamity, but Matt's next words made her sit back down with a thump.

"It looks like Nate is organizing a campaign out there," he said.

"A what?" she asked. "What do you mean?"

"You'll have to see it for yourself," he said. "But it's not going to endear him to the townsfolk. Even though everyone agrees that the mayor was out of line on the eminent domain thing, a lot of the business owners wouldn't mind seeing those townhomes go up to increase business. Now Nate's always been fine to me, so I thought maybe you could have a talk with him. I hear he'll listen to you."

"Oh, for the love of Pete! Nate Williams doesn't listen to me. He doesn't listen to anyone!" Brenna snapped. She was getting sick to death of everyone thinking she had some influence with Nate, especially when what she did have was bubkes.

She brushed some white glue on the back of her apple cutouts and gently stuck them on the side of the ceramic jug. Her fingers were damp from the water bowl and she used them to smooth the apples, being sure to get rid of any air bubbles.

Matt stood watching her, and she knew he was waiting for her to do something.

"Oh, all right," she said. "I'll go see what I can do, but I'm telling you right now, I probably can't do squat."

"Thanks, Brenna," Matt said. "Not for nothing, but this situation between Nate and the mayor is getting a little out of hand."

She washed her glue brush and dried her hands at the sink in the back of the room. Then she grabbed her black backpack purse from under the counter.

"I'll try to talk to him," she said. "Although I'm sure I'll be of no use whatsoever. Tenley, do you mind making sure my apples dry smooth? I'll be back later."

"Sure," Tenley agreed. "Good luck!"

Brenna waved as she let the door swing shut behind her. She wished Matt had given her a better idea of what to expect, but it seemed to be beyond his descriptive capabilities. That had to be bad. What could Nate be up to? Hadn't he caused enough of a ruckus with his sketch of the mayor? What could he have cooked up now?

In exactly four and a half miles, she could stop speculating. Visible from the main road were big, garish yellow signs that read "Save Morse Point Lake!" and "Down with Dim Dipley!" They were planted all over the lakefront property like oversized, monster dandelions.

Brenna felt her jaw do a slow drop and stay there as she gaped in wonder at her front lawn. Nate had obviously lost his mind.

She parked in the small communal lot they all shared and scanned the cabins perched around the lake.

"Brenna!"

She turned to see Twyla, one of Nate's older tenants, skipping, yes skipping, across the lawn toward her. It was quite a sight since Twyla was somewhere in her early sixties. It had taken a few months, but Brenna had grown accustomed to Twyla's skipping. She said it kept her young, and truth to be told, Brenna had actually tried it in the privacy of her own home. She had to agree that there was something invigorating about skipping.

Twyla was a character. She wore her long gray hair in a braid that hung down to her waist and she favored brightly patterned broomstick skirts. The matching tops were usually weighed down with a variety of polished stone necklaces, earrings, and bracelets. She was a sculptor of metal by trade and usually had a welder's helmet perched on her head. Today, however, she wielded a fistful of paintbrushes.

"Hi, Twyla," Brenna said faintly. "Lovely day, isn't it?"

"You're just in time." Twyla grabbed Brenna's hand in her callused one and dragged her across the lawn toward Nate's porch.

The other two tenants, Paul and Portia Cherry, were a married couple who lived in separate cabins because of Paul's snoring. They were sitting on the porch amid cans of paint with brushes in hand. Like Twyla, Paul and Portia were older than Brenna. She guessed them to be somewhere in their fifties. They both wore glasses and kept their gray hair cropped short, as if their years together had caused them to begin to resemble one another. Being roughly the same height and body shape, they reminded Brenna of a pair of bookends.

Childless, they had retired young, Paul from being an economist and Portia from a career in nursing, to pursue their artistic dreams. Portia worked in glass, while Paul's preferred medium was clay. Given that the sight of blood made Paul woozy, they didn't share studio space either. He had been known to faint whenever Portia nicked her finger on a sharp edge.

The couple had just finished another sign and were admiring their handiwork when Brenna and Twyla joined them. This one said, "Keep Morse Point Lake Free!"

The words were bordered by psychedelic swirls of color that were almost blinding in their intensity. Brenna feared there'd be a lot of drivers heading right into the lake if this was placed within eyeshot of the road.

"Isn't it fabulous?" Twyla asked.

"Uh . . . yeah," Brenna agreed. The others looked so pleased with themselves that her underwhelming response went unnoticed. "Is Nate around?"

"He sure is." Twyla looked away from the sign and pointed toward the far side of the lake. "He's putting up a few signs down by the swimming hole. Wait 'til he sees this one!"

On a map, Morse Point Lake looked like a big blue handprint just a few miles from the center of town. It covered 320 acres with one main body of water and several long inlets that ran off into smaller streams and brooks. Nate's cabins surrounded the thumb part of the handprint, and the property he'd been acquiring over the past few years surrounded the main body of water.

The locals' favorite swimming hole was a large sandy beach on the main lake. Nate owned the land, but he let the townspeople use the lake with the stipulation that the town provide lifeguards during the summer. Brenna had not known any of this until a few days ago when the Porter twins had stopped by to swap information. They had been woefully disappointed with what Brenna had brought to the table, which was nothing, but the joy of sharing what they knew overrode their censure.

Brenna followed the path to the main lake. It had rained during the night and left the path riddled with puddles and slick with mud. It squished up the sides of her shoes and she was glad she had worn her cotton sneakers. At least they were washable.

It wasn't long before she could hear the rhythmic banging of a hammer on a stake. As she stepped around a budding maple by the water's edge, she saw Nate in a bright blue T-shirt and jeans bent over yet another sign. This one read, "Impeach Dim Dipley!"

"Hi, Nate," she called.

He glanced up at her and grinned. Brenna blinked. She'd never seen him look so animated before. He wore a self-satisfied smile, the kind you'd expect to find on some-one who was winning an argument.

"Having fun?" she asked.

"Nothing like a good cause to get your motor running," he agreed. He lowered his hammer and stretched his back.

Brenna had to appreciate the way his eyes crinkled in the corners and his lips turned up in an impudent grin. He looked as happy as she'd ever seen him.

Still, Matt had said the local business owners weren't going to be happy with Nate's eye-popping campaign. Given that Matt had lived here all his life, she trusted his judgment. She also knew she should butt out. After all, hadn't she learned her lesson from the last go-around?

And yet, she didn't want to see Nate get into trouble, and not just because it might affect her living arrange-ment. He was an outsider in Morse Point like her, and she felt they needed to stick together. Besides, having lived in a wide variety of apartments in Boston over the years, she knew a good landlord was hard to find.

"You look worried," he said. He tilted his head to the side and studied her. He didn't look amused now. His gray eyes were intent upon her face, making her uncomfortable. She had the feeling he knew exactly what she was thinking. His next words confirmed it.

"The mayor can't do anything to me," he said. "And I'm allowed to have a difference of opinion with him and express it."

"Yes, that's true," she said. "But this is a very small town. Dip . . . er . . . Ripley has lived here all of his life, and you're an outsider."

"Do you think they will tar and feather me? Or run me out on a rail?" he asked. The crinkles were back in the corners of his eyes.

Brenna had no idea why this made her face grow warm. She tried to ignore it. She turned away from him and picked up a long narrow stick. She poked holes in the mud with it.

"What if he succeeds in levying a massive property tax on you?" she asked.

"I can handle it," he said.

"What if they refuse to let you buy any more land?"

"There are many ways to acquire property," he said.

"What if they try to take possession of the cabins again?" she asked. She knew it was a long shot, but she wanted him to understand that this wasn't New York. Memories were long in Morse Point, and unless you were a fifth-generation native-born resident, you might as well be from Mars.

"They won't. No one wants that to become a precedent. I may be an outsider, but no one in this town went for the mayor's attempt at eminent domain, and they never will," he said. His voice was disgusted. "He is the greediest, most corrupt public official I've ever seen. He needs to step down."

She looked at him in alarm.

"Brenna, what are you so worried about?" he asked.

She glanced at him from beneath her lashes. What could she say? He had a self-assurance that she envied, and he was right. He was allowed to have his opinion and express it, even if it wasn't popular with the town officials. She just had a bad feeling about this whole business that she couldn't shake, but how could she explain that to him?

"I just don't want to wake up in the middle of the night and find the villagers marching on us with torches," she said.

He stared at her for a moment and then threw his head back in a great guffawing laugh that was even more contagious than his grin. She laughed, too. She supposed she was being silly. Realistically, what could happen? Nate and the mayor would work this out, sooner or later, and with any luck, it would be resolved in a way that they all found livable.

"Nate!" a shriek sounded from the path, halting their laughter. Twyla appeared in a burst of iridescent blues. "The mayor is on a rampage! Come quick!"

# Chapter 5

For a smooth finish, it is essential to start with a clean and smooth surface.

Nate and Brenna exchanged a surprised look and hurried up the path toward the cabins. Nate took the lead with his longer stride, leaving Brenna to follow, with a winded Twyla bringing up the rear.

"I will not stand for this!" Mayor Ripley shouted. He was jumping up and down on the remnants of one of the signs. The bright yellow poster board was covered in his muddy size nine footprints, and the wooden stake it had been perched on was as splintered as kindling.

"I called the police," Portia shouted from the porch, where she and Paul stood wearing identical expressions of bemusement.

The mayor's head was a bold shade of apple red, his tie was askew, and his suspenders were holding on for all they were worth. When he caught sight of Nate, he gave a primal roar and tugged another sign out of the ground. He

charged across the lawn swinging the sign as if hoping to
smack Nate out of the figurative ballpark with it.

"Was there something you wanted to discuss?" Nate
asked. The mayor kept charging.

Nate gave Brenna a half-stunned, half-amused smile
and jogged over to stand behind the mayor's silver Lexus.
The mayor chased him around the car, but Nate stayed
just ahead of him. With an infuriated grunt, Mayor Ripley
switched directions and so did Nate. This game of tag
went on for several minutes. It would have been funny,
Brenna supposed, if the mayor hadn't been frothing at the
mouth, looking like he planned to shove the business end
of the sign through Nate's heart.

A screech of tires made Brenna turn to look through
the trees that lined the drive to the road beyond. At least
twenty cars had stopped to watch the show, the last one
almost rear-ending the car ahead of it. Several townspeople had climbed out of their vehicles and were sitting on
the trunks, roofs, and hoods to get a better view. If they'd
had coolers and hibachis, it'd look like a tailgate party.

A large white sedan, sporting vintage bubble lights, left
the other cars on the street and wound its way up the
drive. It was a local police car, obvious from the Morse
Point Police Shield on its side, and was being driven by
the chief of police himself.

He parked behind the Lexus and glanced through
his windshield as if unsurprised by what he was seeing.
Brenna knew that Ray Barker had been with the town
police for thirty-five years, and even in an uneventful
town like Morse Point, he had probably seen it all and
then some.

"Gentlemen," he called as he stepped out of his vehicle, "what seems to be the trouble?"

Ray Barker was six foot three, tall and lanky with close-cropped silver hair and a matching mustache that he'd probably had since the seventies. He spoke soft and slow, but Brenna got the feeling that he'd have you splayed out on the ground before you knew what hit you if you gave him any provocation. He was the very essence of law and order.

Chief Barker's gaze slid across the scene, and Brenna knew that he missed nothing from the numerous yellow signs to the two men causing the ruckus to the plump, black and white Muscovy duck swimming for deeper waters in the lake beyond. The chief was cataloging it all. When his gaze rested upon Brenna, she felt her palms get sweaty, which was ridiculous. She hadn't done anything wrong.

Nate and Mayor Ripley abruptly stopped their game of tag. While Nate looked charmingly sheepish, Mayor Ripley was furiously indignant. He threw down the sign he clutched and stomped over toward the chief.

"About time!" he snapped. "Make him take down all of these signs."

The chief just shook his head and spoke in a low drawl that Brenna had to strain to hear. "Can't. It's his property. He can put signs wherever he wants."

"But it's libel, it's slander, why, it's visual pollution!" Mayor Ripley protested. "There has to be an ordinance against this!"

"Well, there isn't," Chief Barker said.

"That can be changed!" Mayor Ripley warned.

"There has been some damage done here, though," the chief said. He gave the mayor a sideways glance. "It could be considered vandalism."

"That is preposterous!" Mayor Ripley protested.

"Did you do this, Mayor?" Chief Barker asked.

The mayor glanced around and Brenna had the feeling he would have lied, but there were too many witnesses.

"I was merely protecting my good name from his lies and propaganda."

"Either way, I need to ask Mr. Williams if he wants to press charges," Chief Barker said.

If the mayor had been angry before, now he looked positively volcanic, as in about to explode.

"Press charges? Against me? Need I remind you that I am the mayor?"

"I think I'm pretty clear on that," Chief Barker said. Brenna could have sworn he had a laugh tucked neatly under his mustache.

She caught Nate's eye over the chief's shoulder and shook her head. Enough was enough. If he brought charges against the mayor, she feared the town really would show up in the middle of the night to burn them out.

Nate glanced away as if he hadn't seen her, and she clenched her teeth. Stubborn man! Why, he made even the most ornery mule seem sweetly dispositioned by comparison. And no, it did not escape her that she was comparing him to a jackass.

"Well, I don't know," Nate said as he leaned against the police cruiser. "Would he have to do jail time?"

The mayor gasped and clenched his fists.

"For a few signs?" Chief Barker asked. "No, 'fraid not."

"Community service?" Nate asked.

"Nope." Chief Barker moved to lean beside Nate. "You're looking at a citation with a minimal fine."

Mayor Ripley looked as if he wanted to yell, but he wisely stayed silent.

"Hardly seems worth the effort then," Nate said.

The chief nodded and said, "Okay, then, you head on home, Mayor, and we'll forget the whole thing."

The mayor's head snapped between the two men, and he pulled himself up to the fullest of his inconsiderable height.

"I'll have your job, Chief Barker," he said.

Ray looked at him, and one of his eyebrows lowered skeptically. "I've been ready to retire for six years, but no one will let me. Be my guest."

The mayor let out a snarl and slammed into the driver's seat of his Lexus. With a spray of gravel, he sped down the lane toward the main road. Figuring that the drama was over with the arrival of Chief Barker, the glut of traffic had begun to move just in time to let him merge.

Chief Barker pushed his hat back on his head and looked at Nate. "I've known Jim since he was a kid, and even then he was a snot-nosed little bugger. But are the signs really necessary?"

Nate shrugged. "He's trying to develop the lake. I'll do whatever it takes to stop him."

"Some folks think development is good for the local economy."

"It'll cause the lake to become overcrowded with water-skiing yahoos and motorboats, and it'll kill off the brook trout," Nate said solemnly.

Chief Barker frowned. "Can't have that. Maybe I should go and take an informal survey of the wildlife."

Nate nodded and it seemed to Brenna that an unspoken understanding passed between them.

The chief went to the back of his car and opened the trunk. He pulled out a rod and reel and a large tackle box. He slammed the trunk, and with a tip of his hat, he disappeared down the path that wound around the inlets.

Brenna gave Nate a questioning look, and he grinned and said, "It's all who you know."

"Indeed," she agreed. She felt like smacking her own forehead. How could she have been worried about him? If ever there was a man who did not need looking after, it was Nate Williams.

# Chapter 6

Usable images can come from such varied sources as wrapping paper, magazines, and paper napkins.

As Brenna learned over the next few days, the town residents were quite divided in their opinions of Nate versus Mayor Ripley and the future of Morse Point Lake.

Two days after the mayor's hissy fit at the lake, she was standing in the checkout line at Mitch's Hardware Store, which sat across the town square from Vintage Papers, buying a large can of Polycrylic for her next class. She was second in line when Mitch the owner and Bart the store clerk, who, thanks to Tenley, she now knew liked to streak across the green to relive 1972, began to have a heated discussion behind the counter.

"He's saving the lake for everyone," Bart Thompson said. He was wearing his usual tie-dye T-shirt, and his long gray ponytail was tucked into his apron.

"He's impeding the growth of the town," Mitch argued. "How do you think I am going to keep paying your salary if we don't get some new residents in this town?"

"You haven't given me a raise in two years," Bart growled. "So I know you're saving money there."

"Tree hugger," Mitch accused.

"Corporate shill," Bart snapped back.

The customer ahead of Brenna hurried through his transaction as if uncomfortable with the sudden tension.

Brenna felt the same way.

Mitch barely glanced at her as he rang up her purchase, and Bart bagged it with more exuberance than was necessary.

She had almost made a clean getaway when Bart called after her, "Hey, don't you live out there on the lake with Nate Williams?"

"Uh, not with him, no," Brenna said. "But I do rent one of his cabins."

"Well, you tell him that I think he's doing the right thing," he said. "Power to the people!"

"Huh," Mitch grunted.

"I'll do that," Brenna said and hurried out of the shop. She found the same debate raging at the post office and the grocery store.

When she stopped by the library to return her books and scan the new book rack, she overheard the head librarian, Lillian Page, talking to Roger Chisholm, the president of the local historic preservation society.

"I do have a book about the history of Morse Point that includes the cabins," she was saying.

Brenna's ears perked up. She had no doubt that they were talking about *her* cabins. She picked up a book and pretended to read the cover blurb.

"Excellent," Roger said. "That should make it much easier to get them designated as a historic site. Oh, I can't wait to see Ripley's face."

Lillian pushed up her narrow, dark-framed glasses and studied him. Wearing a cardigan with patches on the sleeves, Roger had a scholarly look to him, which was reinforced by his thick silver hair and neatly trimmed beard.

"Still bitter, Roger?" she asked, her tone gently teasing.

"Bitter, I'm not . . ." he began to protest and then his shoulders slumped and he sighed. "Yeah, I'm pretty bitter."

They both laughed and Brenna knew they shared a joke to which she wasn't privy.

"I don't blame you," Lillian said. "He maneuvered the town council into buying that land to put that strip mall up before the preservation society could make an offer."

"They just plowed over the old school yard as if it were no more a historic site than the dump. It was such a travesty. Well, I think the mayor has finally met his match. I'm going to enjoy watching Nate Williams take Jim Ripley down," Roger said. "And I'll do anything I can to help."

It seemed to Brenna that Roger Chisholm was more than a little bitter. In fact, it sounded as if should Ripley happen to step in front of Roger's car, he'd be hard pressed to decide whether to hit the gas or the brake.

She left the library with a wave to Lillian, who frequented her decoupage classes, feeling more than a little disturbed. A resolution needed to be made about the lake property, and soon, before the town was irrevocably divided by the issue. She mulled it over on the drive back to her cabin, but with no resolution in mind by the time she got home, she was happy to close her door on the entire mess.

She had bought a fresh loaf of French bread and

quickly pulled together the ingredients for a cheese soufflé, which she seasoned with dry mustard, garlic powder,
and kosher salt. While that baked for thirty-five minutes,
she made a spinach salad with raspberry vinaigrette and
poured herself a glass of wine.

The sun was just beginning its descent so she took her
wine outside. She sat on the top step and rested her back
against the porch railing, watching as the lake reflected
the sky's deepening amber hues as perfectly as a mirror. A
soft breeze sent ripples across the water's surface, and
Brenna wrapped her arms about her middle, trying to keep
in more of her own warmth. This was her favorite time of
day, when the woods surrounding the lake took on hushed
tones like a parent tucking a child into bed.

As the water smoothed back into its pristine veneer,
she saw something bob to the surface. At first she thought
maybe one of Nate's signs had fallen into the drink, but
no. This was too large and too brown.

She placed her wineglass on the top step and rose from
her seat. The sunset was now bursting into vibrant shades
of blood red tinged with gold. She felt a chill spread up
her arms, giving her goose bumps.

She squinted at the object in the water. It looked like an
old wooden steamer trunk. What was it doing in the lake?
Having spent many of her days off foraging in the town
dump, looking for old furniture to restore and decoupage,
Brenna couldn't help but think that this trunk could be
quite a find if it wasn't too water damaged.

Without stopping to reconsider, she kicked off her shoes
and rolled up her pant legs. The trunk was close enough
that she didn't think she'd actually have to swim for it.
She grabbed a fallen tree limb from a nearby willow and
shimmied out onto a big rock at the edge of the water. She

had to use two hands to maneuver the branch over the trunk to try and rake it closer. It bobbed on the water, getting nearer before it got bogged down in the weeds that filled the shallows at the water's edge. Damn.

Brenna debated leaving it there. She loathed the feel of slimy weeds on her feet. But then, what if it had just fallen off someone's truck when they were moving? It could be in excellent condition. She could picture it painted white with deep blue hydrangea blossom cutouts trailing up one side and down the other. No, she couldn't let it sit.

Gritting her teeth, she stepped into the frigid water and waded out to the trunk. Jagged pebbles dug into the soles of her feet, while slippery weeds wrapped around her ankles. Ew. Still, she kept going.

When she reached the trunk, she was delighted to find the burgundy leather handles and brass hardware on it looked to be in good condition. She grabbed the handle and tried to pull the trunk to shore. It was heavier than she'd expected so it had to be full of someone's belongings, making her think someone had indeed lost it by accident. Its buoyancy in the water helped her get it to the edge of the lake, but it took all of her strength to pull it clear of the water. She dragged it onto a patch of grass and collapsed beside it.

She wondered if it was full of blankets. If they'd gotten waterlogged, it would certainly explain why her back was having spasms right now. Maybe it had someone's wedding dress in it. A tingle of anticipation wriggled down her spine. It was as if she'd found a treasure chest, and all she had to do was pop the lid to see what secrets it held.

She climbed up onto her knees and examined the front of the trunk. The latches were easy to unhook, but the flush mount circular lock wouldn't budge. Whoever had shut it had not left the key with it.

Instead of dampening her enthusiasm for her find, the lock only made Brenna more determined to bust it open. After all, she would have to find out who owned the trunk if she had any hope of returning it to them. And how else could she figure that out than to open it and look for clues?

She hurried up to her cabin. The smell of her cheese soufflé distracted her and she stopped to pull it out of the oven before grabbing her toolbox from the bottom of the pantry cupboard and racing back to the trunk.

She chose a flat-headed screwdriver first. It fit into the lock and she jiggled and wiggled it, but nothing happened. Next she chose the smallest of her metal files. It fit into the lock and she pushed it up and to the right until she heard a faint click. The round face of the lock flopped forward and Brenna dropped the file into her toolbox.

The sky was a smoky shade of purple now and she fished in her toolbox for her small flashlight. She turned it on and held the unlit end with her teeth while she grasped each corner of the trunk's lid and slowly lifted it open.

At first, it did look like a bundle of old blankets. No treasure then, she thought. Darn it. But then she noticed the blankets seemed to be wearing an expensive leather belt. She gasped and the flashlight fell out of her mouth and rolled across the grass to plop into the lake. In seconds its little beam was extinguished, and Brenna was left in the encroaching dark with a trunk that she suspected had a body in it.

She felt a scream claw its way up her throat, but she swallowed it. Maybe it was just her imagination, she thought. Maybe it was just a bundle of old clothes. She swallowed hard and forced herself to lean closer to the trunk. Her fingers were shaking as she reached forward and touched the sodden clothes. There was no mistaking the feel of a hard, cold body encased in the wet dress shirt beneath her fingers.

She leapt back from the trunk. Her heart was racing triple time and she flapped her hands uselessly at her sides as she tried to think of what to do. She should run for help, she thought, but what if the person was alive?

In a panic, she dashed forward and began to tug the person out of the trunk. He could be alive. Maybe it was just a practical joke gone wrong. She tugged and pulled but the person was wedged pretty tight. Finally, she reached down and hefted the body up by the armpits and hauled it to a sitting position. Staring back at her with wide vacant eyes was Mayor Ripley. Water gurgled out of his open mouth and Brenna screamed.

# Chapter 7

Make it a hobby to seek unusual papers for decoupage.

Porch lights from the cabins around her snapped on. Brenna was unaware. She felt her stomach churn and she sank into the dirt, putting her head between her knees to keep from throwing up.

Hank, the golden retriever, came bounding down from Nate's cabin, barking all the way. He nudged her face with his cold nose and licked her cheek. The slobber actually felt good in the brisk night air. She felt dizzy, but as she sucked in great gulps of oxygen, she thought she might not hurl.

"Brenna!" Nate came skidding across the grass to where she sat hunched. She was wet, cold, and shaking. "What happened? Did you fall in? Are you okay?"

He slid to a stop, and she noticed he was barefoot. He was wearing jeans, and his shirt was unbuttoned as if he'd been in the middle of changing when he was interrupted. Landing on his knees beside her, he grabbed her arms and forced her to look at him. His gray eyes were searching, as if he were trying to see inside her to make sure she was all right.

Twyla, Paul, and Portia followed in his wake, shouting questions as they hurried across the lawn.

"What happened?"

"Is that Brenna?"

"Is she okay?"

The questions came fast and furious from all sides, but no one seemed to notice the trunk or, more accurately, what was in the trunk.

Brenna felt winded and shaky as if suffering the aftershocks of an earthquake, but she forced herself to speak. "Someone call Chief Barker. The mayor is dead."

She pointed, and all four of them turned to follow the direction her trembling finger indicated. A gasp rippled through them and there were several muted curses. Nate and Portia stepped closer while Twyla and Paul stepped back.

"I'll call the police," Twyla volunteered, and she ran back to her cabin.

Hank crouched next to Brenna, leaning against her. A low growl came from his throat as he kept his gaze on the trunk. Brenna got the feeling he had placed himself beside her to comfort her. She buried her hand in his soft thick hair and held on.

A former nurse, Portia reached in and pressed her fingers on the pulse point beneath the mayor's left ear. She was still for a moment and then she pulled her hand away and shook her head. She leaned in and placed her ear against his chest. Again, she pulled back with a shake of her head.

"He's dead," she confirmed. Both she and Nate stepped back, knowing that there was nothing more they could do.

Nate turned back to Brenna. He put his arm around her shoulders and slowly helped her to her feet. "Your teeth are chattering," he said. "Let's get you up to the house, where it's warm."

Hank flanked her other side and the three of them walked slowly up to Nate's cabin with Paul and Portia following behind them.

Chief Barker arrived in a matter of minutes with two officers as backup. Nate walked him down to the water's edge. He soon rejoined them and they all waited on the porch while floodlights were set up for the state investigator who would be arriving shortly.

Brenna suspected the others wanted to know what had happened, but Nate sat on the padded bench beside her as if putting himself between her and the others to shield her from any questions. She was grateful. She knew the police were going to ask her what happened, and she didn't want to relive it more than once.

After what felt like an eternity, a van arrived with a Massachusetts state seal on the side. Chief Barker greeted the personnel that climbed out of it with a handshake and stood talking to them for a long while.

Twyla leaned hard against the porch rail in an obvious effort to hear what they were saying. But even the sound-carrying powers of the lake water couldn't bring the chief's low voice up to them on the porch, so they waited in silence until the small group broke up and the chief made his way up to the porch, where they all sat.

Nate had gotten Brenna a hooded sweatshirt to wear, and it spoke to her jumbled state of mind that she didn't protest wearing something with an embroidered Yankees emblem on it. Normally, she would have opted to shiver until all of her teeth fell out first.

"I have some questions for you all," Chief Barker said. "Do you mind if I use your living room, Nate?"

"Not at all," he said.

"Brenna, I'd like to start with you."

She had expected as much. She stood on rubbery legs, and walked across the porch with Hank pressed tightly to her side.

"Is it okay if Hank comes, too?" she asked. Her voice cracked, making her sound almost as vulnerable as she felt, if that was even possible.

Chief Barker nodded and Nate gave her hand a reassuring squeeze when she passed by him. She glanced at him swiftly. The intensity in his gaze made her breath catch in her throat, and she realized he was worried about her.

"Thanks," she said and patted his shoulder as she moved past him and through the screen door.

They sat awkwardly across the large coffee table from one another, Chief Barker in a leather recliner and Brenna on the matching brown sofa.

"How are you feeling?" he asked. Casually, he took a small notebook and pen out of his breast pocket.

"Rattled," she said.

"I can imagine," he said. "Now, I know this was a shock, but do you think you can tell me what happened?"

The chief's voice was its usual slow-as-molasses drawl. He had the *r*-dropping accent of a man born and bred in Massachusetts, but he spoke slower than most natives. It was as if he had learned early on in his career to use his voice as a calming tool.

"I think so," she said. He nodded encouragingly at her and she took a deep sustaining breath. She told him about sitting on her steps with a glass of wine and spotting the trunk on the lake. She described hauling the trunk out of the water and then about opening it. The chief never interrupted but scratched occasional notes in his pad. Then she described finding the mayor and screaming. She paused to catch her breath.

"So you were all alone out there until after you screamed?" he asked.

"Yes," she said.

"Who was the first person to reach you?" he asked.

She smiled. "It wasn't a person."

He looked confused.

"It was Hank." She patted the dog's head. "Then Nate, Paul, Portia, and Twyla all arrived."

"What were their reactions?" he asked. His gaze, which had almost never left her face during her recitation of the evening's events, seemed to get even sharper.

"No one noticed the trunk at first," she said. "They all thought I'd fallen into the lake or hurt myself. I had to point the trunk out to them."

He raised his brows and made a note.

"And what were their reactions after you pointed to the trunk?"

Brenna took a deep breath. It was hard to remember. She'd been so focused on not throwing up.

"Twyla ran to call you, Portia and Nate checked to see if he was actually dead, and Paul swore a lot," she said.

Chief Barker nodded as if he'd expected her answer, and she felt as if she'd passed some unspoken test.

"What will happen now?" she asked.

"We'll investigate the scene to see if we can figure out how this happened, the *Courier* will have a field day with the story, and hopefully, in the end we'll come up with some answers," he said.

Brenna nodded. "Chief, can I ask you something?"

"I can't promise you an answer," he said, "but you're welcome to ask me anything."

"Do you think this was an accident?" she asked. She could feel her heart pound in her ears, almost drowning out his answer when he said, "I can't say for sure just yet, but . . ."

"But what?" she prodded.

"But I can't say for sure yet," he said. Whatever he'd been thinking he thought better of saying. Brenna understood that he couldn't really answer the question, but she really wanted someone to tell her it was just a crazy accident, because the alternative, that it was murder, was just unthinkable.

She went back outside to wait while, one by one, each of her neighbors was questioned as well.

It was a dull-eyed crowd of five that watched from the porch while the police worked under the floodlights that were reflected back at them by the smooth surface of the lake.

Twyla made a pot of jasmine tea and everyone had a cup, though no one seemed to be thirsty. The ritual of mixing in honey and milk kept them busy but not nearly long enough.

Brenna had no idea what time it was when the investigators finally rolled a stretcher with a zipped-up body bag to the waiting van. The trunk was put into another vehicle and slowly the floodlights were dismantled. The yellow crime scene tape, however, stayed as a temporary marker.

Chief Barker told them that he would be in touch if he had more questions, but for now they were free to go. An awkwardness fell over the group, and Brenna wondered if, like her, no one was eager to be alone.

Twyla was the first to stand up. She gathered her teapot and cups onto a large wooden breakfast tray that Brenna had decoupaged for her a few months before. It was covered with cutouts of large bunches of grapes in hues of luscious red and luminous purple, and entwined with twisty rust-colored vines and deep green leaves. It was one of Brenna's favorite pieces and she was gratified to see Twyla using it.

"Well, I think some shut-eye is in order," Twyla said.

"You're right," Paul agreed. He shook his head, as if trying to shake off the stupor he was in. He stood and held out his hand to help Portia to her feet. "There's nothing more we can do tonight."

"Do you want us to walk you back to your cabin?" Twyla asked Brenna.

"I'll take her," Nate volunteered before Brenna could answer.

"Oh, all right. Good night then," Twyla said. The three of them walked slowly back to their cabins, calling out their good nights and giving the part of the lake roped off by the yellow plastic ribbon a wide berth.

Brenna rose to her feet. She supposed she could have told Nate that she didn't need an escort, but that would have been a lie.

She had come to Morse Point to leave the violent crime of Boston behind. She had thought she'd left the demons of her past there in the city, but no. Here she was again being terrorized by violent crime. She felt sick to her stomach and wondered if she'd ever sleep again.

Every time she closed her eyes, all she could see was the mayor's bloated face and the water gushing out of his mouth when she sat him up. A shudder rippled down her spine.

"Are you all right?" Nate asked. He moved to stand beside her.

"No, not really," she said.

He draped an arm around her shoulders and pulled her close. The feel of his solid warmth comforted her, and Brenna soaked it up like a dried-out sponge. He kept his arm around her as they walked down the steps and across the yard. She noticed he was steering her away from the crime scene and she was grateful. Hank followed behind them, emitting a low growl when they passed by the lake.

When they reached her front porch, Nate removed his arm and the night's chill crept into his place, enfolding Brenna in its cold embrace. She shivered. Hank trotted up onto the steps and sat beside her.

"Do you want to keep Hank for the night?" he asked.

"Can I?"

"I don't think you have a choice," he said with a rueful smile.

Hank was leaning against her, as if offering his support, and Brenna reached down to rub his ears. Having Hank around would make the night so much more bearable.

"Are you sure you don't mind?" she asked.

"Not at all," he said. "Hank knows who needs him the most. You had quite a scare tonight."

The breeze picked up one of Brenna's long curls, tossing it about her face as if playing catch with it. Nate reached up and tucked it behind her ear. His gaze was full of concern and it warmed Brenna from the inside out.

"I still can't believe it," she said. "How could this have happened?"

"I don't know," he said. "I was no fan of Ripley's—in fact, I thought he was a complete boob—but I sure never wished for this."

"Wished for what?" she asked. She knew what he meant, but she wanted to hear him utter the words. She wanted someone else to say out loud what she was thinking but afraid to say herself.

He met her searching look with his grave gray stare. He didn't look away when he said, "I never wished for his murder."

# Chapter 8

To strengthen thin papers before use, apply a coat of sealant first and let it dry completely.

Brenna woke up to a face full of dog breath. Her eyes peeled open, and she looked to find Hank sound asleep with his head on the pillow next to hers. He was on his back with his paws in the air, the picture of canine contentment. She couldn't help but smile.

The minute she sat up and pulled on her robe, he snapped out of his deep sleep and jumped to the floor. He shook himself from head to tail, as if that was how he woke himself up, and she wondered if she should try it. Maybe another time—she'd had trouble sleeping last night and had a scorching headache. She was afraid any sudden movements might cause her head to roll right off her shoulders.

She shuffled to the kitchen and started to fix coffee. Nothing was right on her planet until she'd downed at least one steaming cup. Hank bounced around her feet and she wondered if he was hungry. Probably.

She opened her frig and looked for something suitable. She supposed she could just let him out so he could go home, but she was loath to give up his company.

She looked at him over the open refrigerator door. "How about bacon and eggs?" she asked. He wagged his tail, and she took it as an emphatic yes.

She set to work while the coffee brewed. She toasted some of the French bread she'd bought the night before. She had no appetite for the cheese soufflé. It didn't reheat well, and for some reason it was linked in her mind to finding the trunk and the mayor. She dumped it in the garbage, knowing it would be a long time before she made cheese soufflé again.

She flipped the bacon and there was a knock on the door. She turned the heat to low and went to answer it. She ran her fingers through her curls as she went, hoping she didn't look as wiped out as she felt but knowing she probably looked worse, like road kill worse.

As she had suspected, it was Nate. Hank got to the door first and was jumping in a circle. Brenna had to grab his collar as she opened the door for Nate.

"Hi," he said. "I brought Hank's breakfast."

Sure enough, he had a big blue bowl in his hand. He set it down on the corner of the porch and Hank dove for it as if he hadn't eaten in weeks instead of hours.

"I was just making him some bacon and eggs," she said.

"If you do that, he'll never leave," Nate said.

"I wouldn't mind," she said, moving aside to let him in. "He's a great dog."

Unlike her, Nate looked great. His wavy brown hair was damp from his shower and he was wearing a charcoal-colored Henley that turned his watchful eyes the shade of wet slate.

"So you like waking up to a blond in your bed?" he teased.

Brenna felt her face grow hot. She supposed she could flirt and say that she preferred brunettes, but she wasn't sure how that would go over and it was too early in the day to make an ass of herself, so she decided to err on the side of caution and ignore his comment.

"You might have mentioned that he's a bed hog," she said. "But at least he doesn't snore."

"No, but when he starts chasing rabbits in his sleep, you have to watch it or he'll kick you right out of the bed."

"Is that experience talking?" she asked. She took the French bread out of the toaster and spread whipped butter on it.

"See this scar?" He pointed to a small jagged white line in the shape of a crescent moon just above his right temple. "Nightstand at three in the morning thanks to Thunder Paws out there."

Brenna winced in sympathy and then laughed. She couldn't help it. There was something charming about a man who let his dog sleep in his bed despite injury to his own person.

The bacon and eggs were done so she loaded up two plates, adding a piece of toast to each. She slid one plate in front of Nate and kept the other for herself.

"Don't tell Hank you're eating his breakfast," she said.

"I'll save him a piece of bacon," he offered.

She poured them each a cup of coffee and they both took a seat at the breakfast bar in her tiny kitchen. Nate tucked into his food as heartily as Hank but with better table manners. As for Brenna, she ate but not with any enthusiasm.

While waking up with Hank had been amusing, it had

also reinforced what had happened the night before. There was no pretending that it was just a bad dream. Mayor Ripley was dead.

Three sharp knocks sounded on the doorframe of her front door and Brenna started. Nate glanced at her.

"Are you expecting company?" he asked.

"No," she said. She wondered if the news about the mayor had spread through town yet. The roosters on the Milsteads' neighboring farm weren't even up yet; surely, the gossip hadn't traveled that fast. "Maybe it's Twyla or the others?"

"I'll go see," he said. He was off his stool and striding toward the door before she could stop him.

Nate opened the door and there stood Ed Johnson, editor-in-chief of the local paper. At the sight of Nate Williams answering Brenna's door, he went rigid as a pointer dog spotting a fallen pheasant.

Brenna resisted the urge to groan. This was all she needed after a night of no sleep.

"Hi, Ed," Nate said. His voice betrayed nothing of what he was thinking. "What can we do for you?"

"I . . . uh . . ." Ed stammered and stuttered. Obviously, he'd been caught off guard by finding them together and by Nate's show of cooperation. It was as if his head was so full of questions that he couldn't pick one to ask.

"Yes?" Nate said.

Ed stared stupidly at the pad in his hand. "About last night," he began, "I have some questions."

"Don't we all?" Nate asked.

"Huh?" Ed looked confused. He glanced over Nate's shoulder at Brenna. "Ms. Miller, is it true that you found the body?"

Brenna felt all the blood rush out of her face. She didn't

want to do this. She didn't want to talk about it. She didn't want to think about it. She didn't want to be known as the poor schnook who'd dragged the trunk out of the lake and discovered the mayor's body.

She especially did not want her name in the paper inviting anything from her past back into her life. She'd left everything in Boston behind her, and she had no intention of letting Ed Johnson write a story about her that would lead a trail to her new life.

From across the room, she could feel Nate's scrutinizing glance. She didn't want to put him in the position of chasing Ed away, but according to the rule of closeness, he was closer than she was so it fell to him. It was a convenient rule.

"Sorry, Ed, Brenna's not up for an interview at this time," Nate said, correctly reading her expression. "You'll have to come back later. And perhaps, you'd better call first."

He went to close the door but Ed shoved the toe of his scuffed leather loafer into the opening.

"You can't refuse me an interview," he said. "This is the biggest story to ever hit Morse Point."

"You're a good writer, Ed, I'm sure you'll manage," Nate said.

"No!" Ed snapped. He pushed against the door with all of his weight, and Nate was forced to brace it with his shoulder to keep him out. "Do you have any idea how long I've waited for this? Do you have any idea of how hard I've worked, of what I've done to get here?"

Brenna rose off her stool and moved to stand behind the counter. The desperation in Ed's voice made her nervous, and she was afraid he would force his way into her house if need be.

Abruptly, Nate relaxed his hold on the door and Ed fell into the room, sprawling across the IKEA area rug in an untidy heap. Before he could scramble back to his feet, Nate scooped him up by the collar and the back of his pants and tossed him out the open door to land in a jumble of arms and legs on the front lawn.

"Have a nice day," Nate said. Then he quickly closed and latched the door and pulled down the shades on all the windows.

"Whoa," she said, impressed.

"I bartended my way through art school," Nate said with a shrug. "I frequently had to toss out the drunks. Nosey reporters aren't that much different, although they do put up more of a fight."

"Thank you," Brenna said. "I know I can't avoid him for long, but I'd like to shower first at least."

Sure enough, a fist pounded on the door again.

"Go away, Ed!" they shouted at the same time.

"I'm not going anywhere until you talk to me," Ed shouted back through the door. Then they heard a low-pitched growl. It was Hank, back from his morning walk and not happy to find a stranger on Brenna's porch.

"Nice doggy." They heard Ed through the door. "Nice doggy."

The growling continued and Ed yelled, "Hey, you want to call him off?"

"Should we?" Brenna asked. Nate didn't seem worried, but she didn't want Ed to sic the dog warden on Hank because of her.

"Nah, Hank won't hurt him, he'll just show him his teeth until Ed gets the message," he said.

The growling continued and they heard Ed step off the porch while still trying to reason with Hank. Brenna crossed the room and peeked around the blind. Ed was hurrying across the lawn to his car while Hank was doing his best impression of a stalking lion.

As soon as Ed drove away, Hank came trotting back to the door, wagging his tail and looking quite pleased with himself. Brenna opened the door and offered him two strips of leftover bacon.

"Good boy," she said, and she scratched his back just the way he liked it.

Nate moved to stand in the open door. "You can shower now," he said. "I don't think Ed will be back for a while."

"Thanks," Brenna said. "I really don't want my name in the paper."

Nate looked at her questioningly and she realized she'd said too much. Before he could ask for an explanation, she said, "What do you think he meant when he asked if we knew what he'd done to get here?"

He studied her for a moment as if trying to decide whether to allow her to change the subject. Finally, he said, "I think he meant covering all of the lousy stories that he's had to write all these years, from school board meetings to charity yard sales. He's finally got hard news and he's not going to give it up easily."

"Oh," Brenna said. She supposed that could be true.

"Why? What do you think he meant?" he asked.

"Nothing," she said.

She wasn't going to admit that she thought he was saying he had done something to create this story. Not yet anyway.

# Chapter 9

Laying out the image is a lot like fitting together the pieces of a puzzle.

It wasn't long after Nate and Hank had left and Brenna had showered that the phone started ringing. Judging by the messages on her voice mail, the gossip had begun at the early bird breakfast at Stan's Diner with the waitress Marybeth DeFalco, who was married to one of the police officers who'd been at the scene. With every order of coffee, she served up a side of the latest dish, today's being the mayor found dead in a trunk. By eight o'clock in the morning, the entire town knew that Cynthia Ripley was now a widow.

Brenna didn't answer her phone and stopped checking her messages. She supposed some people were calling to see if she was all right, but she imagined most of them were looking for information. Well, she didn't have any and she didn't need to relive the whole horrible experience for the vicarious thrills of others. So there.

Once it was more dry than wet, she pulled her curly,

reddish brown hair back in its usual band and put on a moss green sweater, which made her hazel eyes appear more green than brown. She wore tan khakis, and in deference to the mud, she donned her hiking boots instead of her usual sneakers. She locked up her cabin and followed the path to the communal lot.

Although it was her day off, she just couldn't sit on her porch staring out at the lake beyond, thinking about last night. She needed to be in motion. She needed to be someplace where she felt comforted and safe. So she climbed into her Jeep and went to work at Vintage Papers.

As soon as she opened the door, Tenley charged at her from across the room and folded her into a hug that would have suffocated her if it had lasted a second longer.

"Brenna, are you okay? Are you all right? I've been calling and calling. Why aren't you answering your phone? I was just about to drive out to your place. Why didn't you call me last night?"

"Tenley, breathe," Brenna ordered, grabbing her friend by the elbows and pulling her off.

Tenley sucked in a long breath, in through her nose and out through her mouth.

"Okay, I'm better," she said. "Now start talking."

So much for hiding, Brenna thought ruefully. It was all right, however, because it was Tenley. She knew it was concern and not gossip that motivated her.

Tenley flipped the Closed sign on the shop door and locked it. Then the two of them hunkered down in the break room in the back of the shop with a pot of coffee and a box of doughnuts. Brenna could have sworn she wasn't hungry but she managed to eat two jellies and a cruller while she told her tale.

When she got to the part about discovering Mayor Rip-

ley in the trunk, Tenley covered her mouth with her hand
and turned an unflattering shade of green.

"Did you throw up?" she asked from behind her hand.
"I would have thrown up."

"I came close," Brenna admitted. Then she told her
how the investigators were there until the wee hours of
the morning and that Nate had lent her Hank to get her
through the night. She did not mention breakfast with
Nate or how he'd tossed Ed Johnson out that morning.
She figured Tenley already had enough to process as it
was.

"I just can't believe it," Tenley said. "Who would want
to kill Mayor Ripley?"

"You mean other than Nate?" Brenna asked.

Tenley gasped. "You don't think . . . ?"

"That Nate did it?" she asked. "No, absolutely not."

"But you're worried about him," Tenley guessed.

"Nate's like me," Brenna said. "He's not from around
here and he keeps to himself. It would be easy for people
to read bad things into that."

"I wish I could argue with you, but you're right. The
people of Morse Point have long memories," she said.
"And even though Jim Ripley was, well, an idiot, he was
still one of our own and the locals won't forget that."

Brenna nodded. This was exactly what she needed,
someone who understood the situation.

"So if it's not Nate, and we're agreed it's not, then
who?" Tenley asked.

"Cynthia?" Brenna suggested. "Isn't it usually family
that they consider first in a murder?"

"They do, but I don't see it." Tenley shook her head.
"Cynthia made Jim what he is . . . er . . . was. It was her
foot in his behind that got him into politics to begin with,

and I can't see her stuffing her investment into a trunk. Being the mayor's wife gave her the cachet she always dreamt of, and I don't see her letting it go, not willingly at any rate."

The sound of someone banging on the front door interrupted their talk. They glanced at one another, and Tenley stood up and poked her head out the back room door.

"It's the Porter sisters," she said. "And they look like they mean business."

"You don't think they'd actually break down the door, do you?" Brenna asked.

"Let's see, this is the biggest thing that's happened in Morse Point since Louise Holbrook backed over her cheating husband fifty years ago, and I hear Marybeth down at the diner scooped them on this one. That must be sticking in their craw like a lobster claw. So, um, yeah, I could see them tossing a brick to get in."

"Well, don't just stand there, open the door," Brenna said. "I'm pretty sure your insurance policy doesn't cover gossips on a rampage."

Tenley hurried across the room, and Brenna braced herself. She had an ulterior motive for talking to the Porter twins. She wanted to know what the scuttlebutt was in town, and they were just the ladies to tell her. It was going to be the gossip equivalent of you show me yours and I'll show you mine.

Tenley unlocked the door and the two women yanked it open and marched in. Brenna had repositioned herself at the large worktable in the back of the shop. She had a basket of paper cutouts in front of her that she pretended to be sorting.

"Good morning, Ella and Marie," she said. "How are you today?"

"Spill it," Marie said. She was bouncing up and down on the balls of her white tennies, looking ready to bust out one of her karate-for-seniors high kicks if Brenna didn't give her what she wanted.

"Whatever do you mean?" Brenna asked, playing dumb.

Ella gnashed her teeth, and Tenley shot Brenna a worried look. Brenna wondered briefly if she and Tenley could take them. She had a feeling the Porter sisters could rumble, and she'd lay odds they fought dirty.

"You know why we're here," Ella said. "So start talking. What do you know?"

"You first," Brenna said.

"What?" Marie gasped, taken aback. "You were the one who fished him out of the lake, you go first."

"I want to know what the buzz is about town," Brenna said. "I want to know what people are thinking and saying."

The sisters exchanged a long look. They wore matching running suits, Marie in yellow and Ella in green. Their gray hair sprang about their heads in recently tightened sausage curls and they both favored a shiny, bubblegum pink shade of lipstick.

As if reaching an unspoken agreement, they turned back to Brenna, pulled out chairs, and sat down. Tenley went to fetch the remaining coffee and doughnuts while Ella and Marie decided who should go first.

"You go ahead and start," Ella said. "It's your turn."

"You just want to tell the ending," Marie said. "You go first. I want to be the one to finish it."

"You got to finish it last time," Ella protested.

"No, I didn't," Marie argued.

"Yes, you did. You told Jorge Garcia at the flower shop the entire story before I could even say a word."

"Did not."

"Did too."

"Quiet!" Brenna shouted over them. "Now someone start talking or I am taking my information and leaving."

The twins studied one another again. It was a silent argument with a lot of raised and lowered eyebrows and put-out humphs. Finally, Marie nodded.

"Oh, all right, fine," she snapped. "Save the best part for yourself."

Ella gave her a close-lipped smile.

"Okay, it all started with Marybeth DeFalco," Marie said.

"We already know that," Tenley said. "She's married to Officer Stuart DeFalco and he . . ."

The twins gave her identical baleful glares and she stammered to a halt.

"As I was saying," Marie began again, "it started with Marybeth, and let me just say, if she wasn't married to Stuart, she wouldn't know anything about anything. That girl thinks that she's in the know, but really she has no appreciation of the history of Morse Point residents, so how could she possibly know anything about anything? Am I right?"

"Quite right," Ella agreed.

"Anyway, Marybeth told everyone who came into Stan's this morning that you found Mayor Ripley bound and gagged and stuffed into a trunk that was sunk at the bottom of the lake."

Tenley and Brenna exchanged a look.

"Don't forget," Ella prodded Marie. Marie looked bewildered until Ella pointed at her neck.

"Oh, and he had his throat slashed," she said in an overly dramatic dinner theater stage whisper.

"No, he didn't," Brenna said.

The twins blinked at her.

"And he wasn't bound and gagged either," she said.

"He wasn't?" Ella asked. "Are you quite sure?"

"Quite," Brenna said.

"Well, that's disappointing," Marie said.

Tenley gave her a chastising glance and said, "The rumors have obviously gotten way out of hand."

"The trunk wasn't at the bottom of the lake either," Brenna said. "How could I have possibly found it there?"

The sisters gave her perplexed looks.

"So, it just floated to shore?" Marie asked.

"Sort of," Brenna said. "I saw it in the water and pulled it in. It wasn't out far at all."

"That's what we get for believing Ruby Wolcott's mother," Marie said. "Everyone knows she's getting dotty."

"How did Mrs. Wolcott hear about all this?" Tenley asked.

"Well, from her daughter, Ruby, of course," Ella said. "Ruby heard it from Marybeth at the diner."

"And when Mrs. Wolcott, who lives on our street, took that yippy little dog of hers, Hercules, for his morning trot, she stopped by our house and told us. We should have come here first. Everyone knows those hair-perming chemicals Ruby uses at the salon have made her dumber than a bag full of hammers."

"Yes, but she does a nice job with a blue rinse," Ella said.

"Except for that one time when she forgot Linda was under the dryer," Marie said. "Poor thing walked around looking like a blue snowcone for a month."

Brenna felt her right eye begin to twitch. "Ladies, if we could get back to the subject? How are the locals reacting to the news?"

She wanted to know if the townspeople suspected Nate, but she didn't want to say as much.

The sisters exchanged a shrewd look.

"We could tell you that," Marie said.

"Yes, we could," Ella agreed.

"But . . ." Brenna knew there was a but involved here.

"But first tell us exactly what happened," Ella said. "And no glossing over the details either. We need to have an accurate accounting of events before we can give any more information."

Their pink-tinted lips clamped tight in identical mutinous lines, and Brenna knew she'd get nothing more until she showed hers, as it were.

She took a deep breath and told them about seeing the trunk and pulling it out of the water and finding the mayor inside. Both ladies gasped appreciatively. She then told them about talking to Chief Barker and watching the body bag get wheeled away on the stretcher.

Like her recitation to Tenley, she did not tell them about sharing breakfast with Nate or Ed Johnson's appearance. She wasn't sure why she wanted to keep this information to herself. Certainly, there was nothing wrong with eating breakfast with her landlord or borrowing his dog or having him chase away nosey reporters, but it was as if there had been a subtle shift in her relationship with Nate, and until she knew what it was, she didn't want to talk about it, especially to the two biggest gossips in town.

"So, tell me," she said. "What are people saying about the mayor's death?"

Ella and Marie exchanged a triumphant look as if she were a big fat fish on their hook and they were about to reel her in.

"They think—" Marie began, but Ella cut her off.

"Back off, Sister. It's my turn."

Marie sniffed and sat back in her chair with a pout.

"They think," Ella paused, "that your landlord, Nate Williams, did him in."

"But that's ridiculous!" Brenna argued. "Why would he stuff the mayor in a trunk and put him in his own lake?"

"Everyone knows they were arguing about the property," Marie said. "And he did say he would sell that land over the mayor's dead body."

"That's true," Ella said. "Pete Farcas heard them arguing on the town hall steps."

Brenna exchanged a look with Tenley. They had both heard Nate say it, too. Still, she didn't believe, not for an instant, that he'd actually hurt the mayor.

"No. Nate was having too much fun taking on the mayor," Brenna said. "He was enjoying fighting for a cause too much to end it prematurely. He didn't kill the mayor. I know it."

The Porter twins looked at her with matching calculating gazes. "What proof do you have?"

"Excuse me?" Tenley spoke up on Brenna's behalf.

"She sounds awfully sure that Nate Williams couldn't have done it," Ella said. "Is she his alibi?"

The two ladies twittered, and Brenna felt her face grow hot with embarrassment. Honestly, she felt as if she were in junior high.

"Well?" Marie asked.

"He's just my landlord," Brenna said. "But I know he's innocent."

"Well, that's not what Cynthia said to Chief Barker," Marie said, looking smug with this bit of news.

"What?" Brenna and Tenley said together.

"Cynthia told Phyllis two days ago that she told Chief Barker that Nate Williams repeatedly threatened her husband and that Mayor Ripley had been about to get a restraining order against him."

"She didn't!" Tenley gasped.

"She did!" Ella said.

"How do you know this?" Brenna asked, wondering if it was the same source who'd said Mayor Ripley had been bound and gagged with his throat slashed.

"Because Phyllis's maid, Karen Quincey, told Sarah Buttercomb at the bakery, who told us when we went for sticky buns yesterday. That's why everyone thinks he did it."

Brenna felt sick to her stomach. She'd only been joking with Nate about the townspeople running them out of town because they weren't locals and were causing a ruckus with their signs, but now she wasn't so sure. If enough people thought he'd killed Mayor Ripley, they'd have to take him in for questioning and then what would people think?

She stood up, banging her hip against the table in her haste. She had to let him know. She had to tell him that he was suspect number one.

"Where are you going?" Marie asked. She had a knowing glint in her eye that made Brenna squirm.

"Home. I forgot something," she said.

Tenley nodded that she understood, and Brenna snatched her purse from the back counter and raced out the door, leaving the string of bells on the door handle jangling in her wake.

# Chapter 10

Before cutting, make a color copy of the image as a backup. Always respect copyright.

Brenna stepped out onto the sidewalk and felt the unnatural quiet that blanketed the center of town like an unexpected snowfall. People were gathered around the town green in clusters, speaking in hushed tones. It was as if the mayor's murder had left an indelible mark upon the small community, taking away its sense of safety and security and leaving it vulnerable and exposed like an open wound.

She hurried by three ladies, one of whom was Ruby Wolcott, distinguishable because of her platinum beehive, who owned Totally Polished, the salon on the corner, and who had helped spread the misinformation about the mayor. All three ladies turned to stare at her as she pressed her key fob and unlocked her Jeep with a bing.

She heard Ruby say to her friends, "I'm going to get me one of those."

"Yeah," agreed her friend. "And some Mace. I heard you can take down a bull elephant with one blast to the face."

As a former urbanite, Brenna thought she should probably correct this erroneous information, but there was no time. She needed to get back to the lake and see what, if anything, was happening with Nate.

"Well, then surely it could take down a murderer like Nate Williams," the third woman said.

Brenna stopped short as if she's smacked into a glass wall. It was one thing to ignore their misinformation in regards to personal safety devices; it was another to disregard their opinion of her landlord, no, make that her friend.

She spun away from the Jeep and marched toward them. They looked startled to see her coming. She'd gotten last summer's pedicures from Ruby, but hadn't been in much this past winter as manicures were a bit of a waste of time and money, given her propensity for varnish-dried cuticles and paper cuts.

"Nate Williams is no more a murderer than I am," she said, irate.

The three women goggled at her, and she realized that she might appear to be just the teeniest bit deranged.

Ruby stepped forward and looked her up and down. She patted the side of her enormous up-do with her long purple nails and said, "How do you *know* he's not the murderer?"

"I just do," she said. It occurred to her that she would make a lousy defense attorney.

"And we're supposed to take your word for it, because . . ." Ruby's voice trailed off.

"Yeah, why should we believe you?" The woman to Ruby's right, who was wearing leopard skin pants and sported black spiky hair, asked.

"Because I know him," Brenna said. It sounded lame even to her.

"How *well* do you know him?" Spiky Hair asked. There was no mistaking the innuendo in her voice.

The women chortled and Brenna felt her face grow warm.

"Not *that* well," she said through gritted teeth.

"Too bad. He's a fine-looking man," Ruby said.

"I was behind him once in the market," the third woman, a chubby brunette plainer than Ruby and Spiky Hair, said. "And I looked in his cart. It was full of those weird cheeses with the funny names and imported beer."

"You know, if he were a little friendlier, I'd have made a play for him myself," Spiky Hair said.

"He's not very friendly," Ruby said. "I ran into him at Stan's once, and I couldn't get a smile out of him, and I was wearing that cute little periwinkle top I have that always gets smiles."

"Well, he is from New York City," the brunette whispered, as if he came from the other side of the planet.

Brenna hung her head. She did not want to be here gossiping about Nate. She just couldn't stand that people thought he was a murderer because he wasn't local and liked to keep to himself. And she definitely didn't want to know that the other women in town had the hots for him.

She had to get out of here. She forced her lips to go up in the corners in a facsimile of a smile. "Oh, and by the way, they say pepper spray is much better to use than Mace, which is actually tear gas and not as effective."

She spun on her heel and left the women staring after her as she clambered into the Jeep. Well, what could she say? Twelve hours ago, she'd found a dead body and now she was running on virtually no sleep and too many doughnuts. She was not at her best.

The drive out to the lake was short. Upon arrival, she

saw Chief Barker's cruiser parked in the lot. She felt her heart thump in her chest. Would he arrest Nate? Could he?

She slammed the car door, forgetting to lock it, and hurried to Nate's house. She dashed up the steps and pounded on the door.

Hank went into a frenzy of greeting, and when Nate opened the door, the dog launched himself at Brenna before Nate could grab his collar. Luckily, she'd had the foresight to brace her knees and caught his paws on her hip without getting knocked down.

She rubbed Hank's ears and glanced over his head to look at Nate's wrists to see if he'd been handcuffed, but they were unshackled. She felt her shoulders drop down from around her ears with relief.

Chief Barker sat in the kitchen, drinking coffee. He waved at Brenna. He looked as tired as she felt, with purple circles under his eyes and several hours of beard stubble sprouting all over his chin.

"Morning, Brenna," he said.

"Good morning, Chief," she answered as she came into the house with Hank dancing around her feet.

"I was just about to come and find you," he said. "I have some more questions."

"You're welcome to talk here," Nate offered. "I could take Hank for a W-A-L-K."

Chief Barker looked at him with one eyebrow raised.

"Sorry, I have to spell it; otherwise he goes mental," Nate explained.

"Yeah, I had a shepherd like that," the chief said. "Honestly, I could use some fresh air. It's a nice morning; how about you and I go for a W-A-L-K, Brenna?"

"Oh, okay," she said. She glanced at Nate and he nodded, which she took as encouragement.

She followed the chief as he led the way out the door toward the lake, but in the opposite direction from where the yellow crime scene tape still marked off the area.

They walked side by side with nothing but the sound of a giddy flock of red-winged black birds chirping and the breeze rustling the new leaves on the trees for accompaniment.

Finally, Chief Barker broke their mutual silence. "I know you're probably tired of thinking about last night."

"It's like a B movie horror clip, *The Creature from Morse Point Lake*, stuck in a loop in my head," she said, and he smiled.

"I expect it'll be like that until your brain gets tired of it," he said.

They reached a narrow part of the path and were forced to walk single file until they got around the bend and the path opened up again.

The chief waited until she was beside him before he continued. "You've told me about finding the trunk," he said, "and I appreciate your information. What I need to know now is do you remember seeing anyone around the lake over the past few weeks? Did anyone make an unusual appearance?"

Brenna thought about it. "Other than you, you mean?"

A small smile tipped up the corner of his bushy silver mustache. "Yeah, other than me."

"And I can assume we mean other than the mayor?" she asked.

"Yes," he said.

Brenna mulled over the past few days. The previous twelve hours had been an adrenaline-infused haze, and while there were some parts of it she couldn't forget, there were other lapses in time that she couldn't remember.

Unfortunately, anything from the past few weeks fell into the category she didn't remember.

"I don't remember seeing anyone," she said.

He nodded. "So, nothing unusual has happened lately?"

"Other than finding the mayor stuffed in a trunk, no, nothing," she said.

"Brenna, can you tell me where you were the night before last?" he asked. "Say, between six o'clock and midnight?"

She felt her heart thump triple time. She wasn't fooled for one minute by his honey-dipped voice of calm. He wanted to know if she had an alibi!

"I was teaching a decoupage class at Vintage Papers and then I went for drinks at the Fife and Drum with Tenley Morse," she said. She almost told him he could verify that with Tenley, but she thought that might sound too defensive. Because she couldn't seem to stop herself, she did ask, "Why?"

"I'm just trying to account for everyone's whereabouts," he said. "You know the campaign to save the lake was getting pretty heated. I just have to make sure it didn't get out of hand."

"Actually, I had thought it was beginning to calm down," she said. "I can vouch for everyone who lives here. These people are all artists. They do protests, but they don't murder. Twyla's a vegan, for Pete's sake. She can't even scramble an egg."

Chief Barker gave her an understanding smile that did nothing to soothe her flustered nerves. They had reached a small alcove and stopped for a moment to look out at the water. The sun shimmered on its surface as if a fistful of stars had been scattered upon it. While they watched, a fish jumped, making a loud plop as he went back under.

Chief Barker studied the ripples made by the fish as if trying to figure out which way it went and whether or not he had time to go get his rod and reel. He turned back toward the path and Brenna followed.

"Chief, are we suspects?" she asked.

He smoothed his mustache with his thumb and his index finger. Finally, he said, "In a murder, everyone's a suspect."

Brenna gasped. "So, it was murder."

"Well, Ripley didn't conk himself on the head, lock himself in a trunk, and throw it into the lake," he said. Brenna thought it spoke well of the chief that he didn't add "duh" to his sentence.

So, the mayor had sustained a head injury. Her mind flashed on the sight of him in the trunk. She remembered that the left side of his head had been swollen near his temple. At the time, she had just assumed it was bloated from being under water, but an injury made more sense.

"I guess I knew that," she said. "Did the head injury kill him?"

The chief looked as if he'd recant, but then thought better of it. "Someone clobbered him on the temple," he confirmed. "But we don't know yet if it was the cause of death. I'm sorry. This must be bringing back some bad memories for you."

Brenna tripped over a root, but he caught her by the elbow before she landed on her knees. He pulled her up to her feet and she felt her face become uncomfortably hot, and not because she'd just tripped.

"How long have you known?" she asked. She didn't even attempt to bluff.

"Since you arrived," he said. "I make it my business to keep tabs on the big-city crimes, just in case something spills into my town. I recognized your name from a piece in the *Boston Globe*."

"You never said anything," she said.

"It's not my business," he said. "You were proven to be a victim, not a criminal. I respect your privacy."

"So, why mention it now?" she asked. She was unsure of how she felt about anyone knowing what had happened to her in Boston. Other than Tenley, she'd never told a soul.

"Because I don't want you to think that Morse Point is like that," he said, looking chagrined. "I don't want you to think you're not safe here."

His gaze was sincere, and Brenna found herself feeling unaccountably choked up. She nodded, and through the knot in her throat, she said, "Thanks, Chief. I appreciate that."

They walked the rest of the way back to Nate's house in silence, and Brenna felt oddly better. It was as if Chief Barker had known exactly what she feared, that no place was safe. That Morse Point was just as dangerous as Boston. But it wasn't.

Someone had murdered the mayor for a purpose of their own. It wasn't a random act of violence. And if she wanted to feel safe again, then Mayor Ripley's murder needed to be solved.

And it wasn't just her peace of mind that hinged on a closed case; it was also Nate's freedom. The townspeople seemed to think he had the most to gain by Ripley's death, and given their tiff over the lake, it wasn't that out of bounds. But Nate wasn't a murderer. Brenna knew that as surely as she knew the Red Sox were going to be in the World Series again.

"Chief Barker, may I ask you something?" she asked.

"As always, yes, but that doesn't mean I can give you an answer," he said.

The path narrowed and they walked single file. When it widened again, Brenna moved beside him and asked, "What happened to the trunk?"

"It went to the state crime lab in Sudbury," he said. "They'll be testing it for any trace evidence."

"What will happen to it when they're done?"

"Well, it's evidence, so once they're done examining it, it will go to the property bureau until the prosecuting attorney releases it to its rightful owner, if we ever figure out who that is. Why?"

"Find the owner of the trunk, find your murderer," Brenna said.

Chief Barker threw back his head and laughed. "I wish it were that simple, but I have a feeling if you checked every attic in Morse Point, you'd find one or even two steamer trunks just like it. Those babies were built to last and people have them forever."

"Then maybe we need to look for an attic that's missing one," Brenna said.

"And were you wanting me to deputize you right here and now?" he asked with one eyebrow raised.

Brenna felt her cheeks get hot again. "Sorry," she said. "I don't mean to tell you what to do. I just want the case solved, you know?"

He nodded. "I know. And don't you worry. This is the first murder to hit Morse Point since the Holbrook murder fifty years ago. I have no intention of letting it go unsolved."

Brenna believed him. He spoke with the vehemence of someone who took it personally that something so heinous had happened on his turf, and Brenna had no doubt that he wouldn't rest until the murderer was caught.

As they rounded the bend in the lake, they were within view of the cabins. Brenna started when she recognized the buxom blond standing at the foot of the stairs that led up to Nate's cabin.

"You are a murderer, Nate Williams!" Cynthia Ripley screeched. "You killed my husband, and I am going to see you pay!"

# Chapter 11

To give the cutout a beveled edge, angle the blade of the scissors or knife to the outside of the picture.

Chief Barker broke into a run and Brenna was right behind him. As they reached the cabin, they found Nate standing on the top step of his porch, with his arms crossed over his chest, looking at Cynthia with a mixture of chagrin and annoyance.

Upon closer inspection, Brenna noted that Cynthia wasn't up to her usual immaculate standards. Her hair was flat on two sides as if she'd forgotten to fluff those parts. And her makeup seemed uneven, as if she'd gotten distracted while putting it on and never quite finished.

She was standing beside the chief's car, wearing purple Capri pants, a flouncy red silk blouse, and white chunky heels. Nothing matched. It wasn't a good look.

Chief Barker darted forward while Brenna moved to stand beside Nate.

"Everything okay?" she asked out of the corner of her mouth.

"Peachy," he replied, mimicking her corner-of-the-mouth speech. Brenna suspected he was mocking her, but she decided to let it go.

"Cynthia, what are you doing here?" Chief Barker asked. His voice was soft but stern.

"He killed my husband," she said. She pointed over the chief's shoulder at Nate. "And I want you to lock him up—now."

"How about I give you a ride home?" Chief Barker said. "You shouldn't be driving like this."

"What's that supposed to mean?" she snapped. Her eyes narrowed and her mouth thinned, giving everyone a good idea of exactly how wrinkled she'd be if she hadn't Botoxed herself to a waxy sheen.

"Cynthia, you're getting all worked up," Chief Barker said. "Now I don't have any evidence that Nate harmed Jim. I can't just haul him in because you've decided he's the murderer."

"But he is," she argued. Her jaw was clenched, making it hard to understand her. "I told you he threatened him. He said he was going to kill him!"

"Saying and doing are not the same thing," Chief Barker said. "Believe me, we'll find out who did this to Jim and we'll bring them to justice. I promise."

Cynthia looked wild-eyed at him. This did not seem to reassure her at all.

"I'm telling you it's him!" she shrieked. "And if you won't see that he's arrested, I'll find someone who will."

She stomped away and climbed into her black Cadillac Escalade. To his credit, Chief Barker did try to stop her, but she slammed the door before he could grab it and threw the oversized vehicle into reverse. The chief had to jump clear or risk becoming a speed bump.

"I'd better follow her and make sure she causes no harm," he shouted over the roar of her engine. He hustled to his squad car and gave Brenna and Nate a wave before he drove off after her.

The April morning had become unseasonably hot, and Brenna pushed the sleeves on her sweater up above her elbows. She could hear the hum of a lawn mower off in the distance and smell the scent of fresh-cut grass in the air.

"Iced tea?" Nate offered.

"Yes, thanks," she said.

She followed him into the kitchen, thinking this might be the perfect opportunity to tell him what the townspeople were saying, although he had to have a pretty good idea after Cynthia's tirade. Not that she thought for a moment that Nate gave a damn what anybody thought about him, but still, he should know.

She sat on a kitchen stool and ran her fingertip along the grout groove in the tile, while she tried to figure out what to say.

"Nate." She said his name and then ran out of air.

How exactly do you tell a person that people think he is a murderer? She was pretty sure Emily Post did not cover this one.

"Yes?" He was pouring iced tea from a pitcher into two glasses on the counter. Then he took a lemon out of a nearby fruit bowl and sliced it into fat juicy wedges. He put one in each glass.

"Um, are you aware . . . ?" she stalled again.

"That everyone thinks I floated Ripley into the lake?" he asked. He put down the knife and ran a hand through his hair. Brenna noticed it stood up in spots, making him look younger than he was.

"Well, yeah," she said.

"I figured," he said with a shrug. He took a plastic bag out of a drawer and began to bag the rest of the lemon wedges. "When I was at the Park and Shop, I noticed it was a little frosty in there, and I wasn't in the frozen food section."

Brenna smiled. She had to admire his unconcern, but then he had lived here longer. Maybe he didn't feel the need to belong as much as she did.

"It doesn't bother you?" she asked.

"Let me ask you this," he said. He looked up from the bag of lemons and met her gaze. Again, she was aware of having his complete attention focused upon her. She felt as if the entire world could collapse around them and he wouldn't even notice because he was so intent upon her. "Do you think I killed him?"

"No, of course not!" she said.

He looked away from her with a small smile. "Then no, it doesn't matter to me what anyone else thinks."

She ducked her head, feeling flustered by his gaze and his words. She didn't know what to make of his answer. Was he saying that he only cared what she thought? When she glanced back up at him, his face was inscrutable. How very annoying.

"Now can I ask you something?" He put a glass of tea in front of her. "Something I've been wondering about for a while now."

"Sure," she said. She was pleased that her voice sounded calmer than she felt.

"Why did you move to Morse Point?" he asked.

He came around the corner of the counter and sat on the stool beside her, his knee brushing hers. She watched him take a long sip of his tea and wondered if sleep deprivation was beginning to make her delirious, because this was not the Nate Williams she knew. The Nate Williams she had come to know over the past year shared a love of sweets and baseball with her, and they never deviated from those two topics. Ever.

Then again, they had never shared the discovery of a dead body either, so perhaps this was normal. Not having shared the discovery of a dead body with anyone before, Brenna really couldn't say.

She did know that she was dangling on the ragged edge of exhaustion. Feeling like a frayed carpet, she didn't have enough reserves to knit herself back to coherency. She wasn't sure how much she wanted to share about her past, so she decided the best defense was a good offense.

"For the same reason as you, I imagine," she said.

"Really?" he asked. He turned to study her and his eyes were amused. "You found yourself the center of an art scene you no longer believed in with every sycophantic boot licker in town trying to chisel out a piece of your soul to sell to the highest bidder?"

"Is that what happened to you?" she asked. Her voice was soft even to her own ears, as if she didn't want to scare him off by saying the wrong thing.

"Among other things," he said. "Mostly, I woke up one day and saw a man in the mirror that I didn't like very much, so I knew it was time to make a change."

Ah, so there was more. Brenna considered her words carefully. Obviously, they weren't going for full disclosure here, but it was the first time Nate had ever mentioned his past and she wanted to reciprocate.

"I didn't like the person I saw in my mirror either," she said. "But for me, I was just tired of being afraid. In Boston, I found I was always looking over my shoulder. It was exhausting."

"Why were you afraid?" he asked. His voice was as soft as hers had been, as if he was afraid of scaring her off as well.

"The crime," she said, opting to remain unspecific. "There was too much crime."

"So naturally, you relocated to a place that just suffered its first murder in how long?" he asked with a sideways glance.

"Fifty years, or so I hear. Apparently Louise Holbrook backed over her husband with his powder blue Buick when she caught him cheating. I sure can pick 'em," she agreed and returned his look.

She took a long sip from her glass. The lemon was tart on her tongue against the tea's honey sweetness.

She was enjoying these moments with Nate probably more than she should. It would not do for the sanctity of their landlord-tenant relationship for her to develop a misguided crush on him. But even as she thought it, she feared it might be too late.

# Chapter 12

Fine cutting is the key to decoupage, making a good pair of scissors the most important tool.

Tenley marched into Vintage Papers the next morning with a coffee from Stan's Diner in each of her hands and the *Morse Point Courier* rolled up under her arm.

"Just wait until you see this," she said. "It's outrageous."

Brenna put down the Fiskar scissors she was using to cut out a print of an antique hot air balloon. She was planning to decoupage it onto an old metal letter box, but it could wait if Tenley had news.

Tenley put down the coffees, unrolled the paper with a flourish, and plopped it in front of Brenna. The headline was a scandal by itself but the photo below it made it damning.

MURDER SUSPECT NATE WILLIAMS HAS HISTORY OF VIOLENCE! The bold typeface screamed across the top of the paper. Below it there was a picture of Nate, looking decidedly angry and several years younger.

He appeared to be walking out of a New York City police precinct with a stunning blond beside him. Unable to stop herself, Brenna scanned the article. After a few paragraphs, she felt dirty and it wasn't just the black newsprint residue on her fingers. And yet, she read every word.

Several sources, from self-proclaimed friends of Nate's to maids working at hotels where he'd once stayed, reported to have seen his notorious artistic temper. The photo of him leaving the precinct was purported to have been taken after he and the blond were arrested for trashing their hotel room after a wild party. Lovely.

The reporter for the *Courier*, Ed Johnson himself, speculated that Nate Williams suffered from anger issues. The article went on to speculate that perhaps when Mayor Ripley had crossed him, Nate Williams had finally given in to his violent ways. Ed Johnson ended the piece by declaring that he, too, had suffered at Nate's hands while trying to interview sources for this story. Brenna shoved the paper away, disgusted.

It was her fault. If Nate hadn't tossed Ed off her front steps, Ed wouldn't be coming after him like this. Her stomach twisted at the thought.

The bells jangled on the door and in walked Cynthia Ripley. She looked more put together today than she had in front of Nate's cabin, but just barely. She wore jeans and a pink hooded sweatshirt. Her hair, which was usually shellacked to perfection, was pulled back by a wide black headband, as if she couldn't be bothered to style it.

Although she did seem calmer, Brenna flipped the newspaper over just in case the sight of Nate's photo set her off.

She was carrying a large box, and Tenley hurried over to take it from her.

"Cynthia, how are you?" she asked as she placed the box on the worktable.

"Managing," Cynthia said. Her voice was subdued and Brenna found herself feeling sorry for her. Like her or not, Brenna couldn't imagine how horrifying it must have been to have her husband's dead body found in a trunk in the lake. Poor Cynthia.

"I'm planning the memorial for Jim," she said. Her voice wobbled a bit with emotion, but she pressed on, "And I was wondering if you, Brenna, would be willing to create a memory collage for me to put out at the service."

"Uh . . . sure," Brenna said. Caught off guard, she didn't see how she could refuse.

"Thank you," Cynthia said. Her chin quivered and she opened the box she'd brought with her. "I thought you could decoupage these photos and news clippings onto a plaque to put on display at the service. What do you think?"

Brenna was speechless, but Tenley put her arm around Cynthia and said, "I think it's a lovely idea."

A single tear rolled down Cynthia's cheek, and Brenna felt her own throat get tight. She realized she didn't know what sort of relationship the Ripleys had, but there was no mistaking Cynthia's suffering.

"It's all in here," Cynthia said. She reached into the box and pulled out a manila folder full of clippings. "You don't have to use them all. I'll defer to your artistic vision, but the highlights like our wedding photo and the day he was sworn in as mayor would be critical."

Brenna nodded. She glanced into the box to see if there was more, but the only thing left was the birdhouse Cynthia had decorated two weeks ago.

"Oh, and I was wondering if you could fix my birdhouse?" Cynthia asked. Her voice cracked and now the tears were running down her face in a stream. "I was holding it when Chief Barker told me about J—Jim and I dropped it."

Brenna pulled the house out of the box and noticed the corner did appear to be mashed. It was easily fixable.

"There is an oak tree beside Jim's plot, and I thought I could hang the birdhouse in it to keep him company," Cynthia said. Her voice was barely audible through her sobs, and she turned and wept into Tenley's shoulder.

"Absolutely," Brenna said. She wished she could do more to help. "A little wood putty and paint and it'll be as good as new."

"There, you see?" Tenley said as she patted Cynthia back. "Brenna will take care of everything."

Cynthia straightened up and took the tissue Tenley offered. She sniffed a couple of times and then drew in a shaky breath.

"Thank you both so much," she said. "I'd better go. I have to meet with the florist. I'm having them re-create my wedding bouquet for the wreath for Jim's coffin."

"Are you sure you're all right?" Brenna asked.

"Could I get you some coffee or tea?" Tenley added.

"No, no, I'm fine," Cynthia said. She walked toward the door, dabbing at her eyes as she went. "Now that his murderer is in custody, I can move on with the grieving process."

"What do you mean?" Brenna asked. She felt all of the hair on her arms rise up in alarm.

Cynthia opened the door and the bells jangled again. Standing in the doorway, she turned to face them. The tears on her cheeks seemed to evaporate as she lifted her chin in vindication. "Didn't you hear? Chief Barker arrested Nate Williams this morning for murdering my husband."

The door shut behind her, and Brenna and Tenley exchanged wide-eyed looks of shock.

"It's not true," Brenna said. "Nate didn't kill Jim Ripley. I know he didn't."

Tenley gave her a worried look then her eyes widened again and her mouth formed a small *oh*.

"You like him," she said.

Brenna pretended to misunderstand and said, "Of course I like him, he's a very nice man."

"Oh, no, don't even try it." Tenley shook her head. "You get a goopy look on your face whenever someone says his name. You *like* Nate Williams."

"Well, you should know that goopy look," Brenna retorted. "You get the same one every time Matt Collins walks into a room."

"Ah," Tenley gasped and clapped her hands to her cheeks.

"Ha! Busted!" Brenna said. "I knew there was something going on between you two."

"No, no there isn't." Tenley turned away from her. Her back was stiff as if to ward off a blow, and Brenna feared she'd gone too far and offended her friend.

"Look, Tenley, I'm sorry," she said. "I overstepped. If I admit that yes, maybe, I like Nate Williams just a teeny bit, will you forgive me?"

Tenley spun around with a grin and said, "I knew it!"

"Hey, you tricked me," she protested. "I thought you were mad at me."

"I could never be mad at you," Tenley said with an eye roll that bespoke exasperation. "Honestly, don't you know me by now?"

"Apparently not," Brenna said. "Since I am quite sure there is something happening between you and Matt and you've never mentioned it to me."

"No, there's nothing," Tenley said with a dismissive wave.

"Oh, come on. I just admitted that I like a man in jail," Brenna prompted. "You can't pull the fifth on me now."

Tenley looked uncomfortable. "Oh, all right. You know we dated in high school."

"Yes," Brenna encouraged her.

"But we had a really bad breakup," Tenley said.

"What happened?"

"I dumped him, because my family didn't think he was good enough for me, and when it got serious, they refused to let me see him anymore and like a fool I went along with it," she said. Her voice snapped like a whip, as if she were trying to lash herself with the words that obviously still caused her much pain.

"I'm sorry," Brenna said.

"It gets worse," Tenley said. "I took up with Steve Portsmyth, Phyllis's nephew. He was a big football hero, handsome but dumb as a brick and mean as a snake. He took every opportunity he could to stick it to Matt. It was awful, and I did nothing to stop it. I don't think I can ever forgive myself and I can't expect Matt to either."

Brenna frowned. It seemed to her Tenley's parents should be the ones asking for forgiveness, but she knew that was as likely as the Porter twins giving up gossip.

Tenley's relationship with her family was strained. Although they lived in the same town, Tenley rarely saw her parents. They had expected her to be married to a doctor or lawyer by now, like her sisters, and starting up her own business had put a severe crimp in their plans for her. Of her three sisters, all living in surrounding towns, only one had bothered to come and see her new store. Brenna knew it hurt Tenley deeply, although she seldom talked of it.

"So, like I said, there's nothing between me and Matt," Tenley said.

Yeah, right, she thought. Brenna had noticed that Tenley always wore a cute outfit on Fridays, when they went for their wine and salads at the Fife and Drum, and she was always sure to touch up her makeup beforehand, too. She may say she'd given up hope on Matt, but her actions demonstrated otherwise.

Brenna remembered the day Matt had stopped by the shop to tell her about Nate's campaign. There had been enough sparks between them to start a fire. Tenley was wrong. Whatever was between them, it was anything but nothing.

"Enough about me," Tenley said. "What are we going to do about Nate? Do you really think they've arrested him? Should we call over to the jail and see if he needs bail?"

"I'm sure he has a lawyer," Brenna said. "And I don't know if he'd want us interfering. I just wish I knew what was going on. Who can we call to find out what's happening at the jail?"

"Matt has a cousin who works as a desk clerk over there," Tenley said.

"Well, isn't that convenient?" Brenna asked. "Call him."

Tenley looked unsure.

"Call him," she said again. "This is a matter of life and death."

Okay, perhaps that was a bit over the top, but it got

Tenley over her nerves and over to the cordless phone on the counter. With any luck, Matt would be able to tell them what was happening at the jail and then she could decide whether or not to panic about Nate.

Matt stopped by the shop as soon as he had spoken to his cousin. Now that Brenna knew about the rocky history between them, it was hard not to notice the way Matt's eyes softened when he looked at Tenley. Oh, yeah, there was unfinished business there all right.

Matt's news was good. According to his cousin Janet, Nate had not been arrested but he had been brought in for questioning.

"They let him go just a few minutes ago, after the formal questioning," Matt said. His blond hair fell over his forehead in a becoming way, and Brenna noticed Tenley watching him from beneath her lashes.

"Did he go home?" Brenna asked. She wondered if she should go and offer him some support. He had to be unhappy that he was Chief Barker's prime suspect. It was just so wrong.

"Brenna, I just have to ask." Tenley paused and looked down at the worktable where they were sitting, as if trying to figure how to say what she wanted to say, but Brenna was ahead of her. "You want to know if I have considered the possibility that Nate is the murderer, right?"

"Um . . . well . . . yeah," she admitted.

"I have no proof except for my gut feeling that Nate is innocent," Brenna said. "But I can't see him as a murderer—not now, not ever. It wasn't him."

"Well, I, for one, am glad to hear you say that."

All three of them spun around to look at the back of

the shop. Standing in the doorway to the store room was Nate.

A small smile played upon his lips as his gaze met Brenna's. She tried to ignore the happy flutter she felt as he strolled into the room and took a seat at the large table with them, but it was impossible not to return his smile. She was just so relieved to have him here and not in jail.

Tenley, on the other hand, looked mortified. "I'm sorry, Nate, I just—"

"Had to ask," he said. "I know. I'd have done the same if the situation were reversed."

She looked relieved and then a little piqued. Matt saw her expression and laughed. She playfully punched him on the arm and he stifled his chuckle.

"I hope you don't mind my using the back door," Nate said. "I'm having a little difficulty getting out of town."

He pointed to the front window and they turned to see a crowd of reporters gathered in front of the police station, which was a diminutive building that sat beside the town hall.

"Are they all here for you?" Brenna asked. There had to be fifteen reporters out there, from newspapers as well as TV stations.

"Yep, the paparazzi have landed," he said. "Thankfully, Chief Barker let me slip out the back while my attorney went out the front into the feeding frenzy. I'll probably have to give him a bonus for that. I haven't felt this hunted since I left New York."

"You're welcome to crash with me if you need to," Matt offered.

"I appreciate that, but I called Paul out at the cabins and he's moving Hank and some of my belongings into the vacant cabin next to yours, Brenna. They had a pack of reporters out there, too, so they had to distract them in order to move some of my things."

"How did they manage that?" Brenna asked.

"Apparently, Twyla borrowed my clothes and dressed up as me. Then she took Hank and my truck and headed west on Route 20. I guess they were three towns out before the reporters caught on."

They all laughed, but it quickly faded as the gravity of the situation sank in. Nate was very much a marked man.

"Do you think they're going to arrest you?" Brenna asked.

"I don't know," he said. "But given that Ripley and I had some very public differences of opinion, and the fact that I don't have an alibi that can be corroborated by anyone but Hank, it doesn't look good."

"We have to find out who did it," Brenna said. "And I know exactly where to start."

"You have someone in mind?" Nate asked.

She flipped over the paper and pointed to the article about Nate. "Ed Johnson."

# Chapter 13

Short snips will leave jagged edges. Use longer-bladed scissors and feed the paper into the blades.

Nate's face darkened as he took in the photo and the article.

"This is the trouble with a misspent youth," he said. "It never goes away. Am I correct in assuming that Ed neglected to mention that I was cleared of all charges? That I wasn't even in the room that night?"

"You're correct," Brenna said. She bit back the urge to ask about the blond, but just barely.

"But why Ed?" Matt asked Brenna. "Why would he harm Ripley?"

"He's been waiting for a story like this his entire career," Brenna said. "Maybe he got tired of waiting and decided to create one himself."

"But murder?" Tenley asked. "That's pretty extreme, even for a badger like Ed."

"Anything is possible," Nate said. "But it does seem to be a stretch."

"What about Roger Chisholm?" Brenna asked. "He's the president of the historic preservation society. I heard him talking to Lillian Page, the librarian. It was obvious that there was no love lost between him and Ripley."

"But murder?" Matt asked.

They were all silent, contemplating this possibility.

"Who else then?" Brenna asked, feeling exasperated. If they could come up with a viable list of suspects, surely that would help Nate combat the bad publicity he was getting in the *Courier*.

"Does it matter?" Nate asked, sounding weary. "Ray is on it. I know he won't rest until he catches the killer."

"What if he doesn't?" Brenna asked.

"He will," Nate said. "I trust him."

"I like Chief Barker, too," she said. "But he's only one man. If the media and the town turn against you, well, you could be arrested for a crime you didn't commit."

"The media is notorious for being wrong," Nate said. "And what do I care if the town turns on me? I didn't kill Ripley."

"I know, but . . ." Brenna's protest trailed off as Nate rose to leave.

He tipped his head as he studied her. "You worry too much. Just leave it be. Everything will be okay, I promise."

She watched as Nate slipped out through the back door with a wave to them all, back to his isolated life on the lake.

For a worldly artist, he was so naïve. He really thought that Ray would catch the murderer and his place in the town would resume. He didn't realize that once tainted as a suspect, a person had a hard time shaking off the insidious suspicions of others, even when proven innocent. She didn't want to see Nate suffer through that. The sooner Ripley's real murderer was caught, the better.

"Uh-oh," Tenley said.

"What?" Brenna asked.

"You've got that look in your eye."

"What look?"

"The one that says you're not going to listen to a word Nate says and you're going to do exactly as you see fit," Tenley said.

"That's a look?" Brenna asked.

"Oh, yeah, it's the same look you give me when I try to get you to drink decaf," Tenley said with a smile.

"I'm thinking Ripley wasn't going to develop the lake property on his own," Matt said, breaking his contemplative silence. They both turned to look at him.

Brenna nodded. "I bet you're right."

"Maybe the deal went sour when Nate kicked up a fuss and Ripley's partner held him responsible," Matt said.

"And killed him?" Tenley asked.

"Money is a big motivator," he said.

"How can we find out who he was working with?" Tenley asked. She pulled the leftover snacks from yesterday's class out of the minifrig in the storeroom and passed them around. Both Matt and Brenna helped themselves to a bunch of green grapes.

"We could ask Cynthia," Matt suggested. "She must have known what her husband was doing."

"Maybe or maybe not," Tenley said. She swallowed a grape before she continued. "I'm betting our answers are in his office. If he had an appointment book or a Rolodex or a record of his phone calls, it might lead us to whoever he's been working with. The question is, have the police taken it all as evidence, and if not, how do we get access?"

Tenley and Brenna exchanged a look. The box Cynthia had dropped off sat on the table between them.

"I think I have an idea," Brenna said. She tapped her chin with her forefinger. "Cynthia has asked me to make a memorial plaque for Ripley's service. I could stop by his office and ask his secretary if there is anything from his office that should be included and use the opportunity to search."

Matt looked impressed. "That just might work."

"Unless the police have already confiscated everything worth taking," Tenley said.

"Yes, but this will give us an opportunity to look around at least," Brenna said. "Who is his secretary?"

"Eleanor Sokolov." Matt and Tenley said it at the same time with identical expressions of distaste.

"What's wrong?" Brenna asked.

"She's a dragon," Matt explained. "She used to be the office secretary at Morse Point High School. Put one toe out of line and that woman would have you in the principal's office so fast you didn't even have a chance to think up a good lie."

He and Tenley exchanged a look ripe with memories, and Brenna looked away, feeling as if she were intruding on their shared history.

"We'll need a distraction," she said.

"And a lookout," Tenley added. Her cheeks were flushed and her eyes sparked. "I want in. I owe that old busybody some payback."

"Me, too," Matt said. "Let me provide the distraction."

"No. I don't even like the idea of going in there myself," Brenna said. "The only reason I'm considering it is because I have a solid reason to be there. I can't let anyone else get swept up into this mess."

Tenley looked down her nose at Brenna with her best Morse family look of disdain. "I'm sorry, Ms. Miller, but what makes you think you have any choice in the matter? I am a Morse, and I do as I please."

"Whoa, you look just like your mother," Matt said.

Brenna was hard pressed to decide if he was more impressed or intimidated.

"I can do a pretty good Tricia Morse when I want to," Tenley admitted in her mother's voice. Then she grinned and her entire persona changed back to the Tenley everyone knew and loved.

Matt blinked and Brenna laughed. Tenley seldom used her prominent family status to coerce people, but when she did, it was a sight to behold.

"You might as well give in," Matt warned her. "Her mind is made up, and you will need a lookout. Besides, I owe Ms. Sokolov some payback, too. You can't deny me."

Brenna was thoroughly exasperated as she looked at the two of them. "You do realize you could land in a heap of trouble, possibly even jail?"

They nodded, with much more enthusiasm than she liked.

"Fine," she said with a put-upon sigh. "Let's get planning."


Brenna tried to shake off her nerves as she and Tenley approached the town hall, but it was impossible to ignore the sheen of sweat coating her palms, and she wiped them on her pants as they climbed the main steps.

"Okay, remind me again," she said. "What are the keywords I'm looking for?"

"Anything with the name or phone number of the developer Ripley was working with," Tenley said. "Look for things that sounds corporate or incorporated or limited liability, blah, blah, blah."

"Okay, I've got it," Brenna said. "And you'll be right by the door doing lookout duty."

"Yep, me and Eleanor are going to have some fun. Well, I am at any rate," Tenley said

They passed through the massive columns that led to the front door, and Brenna realized she had never been so intimidated by a building before. The Morse Point Town Hall had been built by Tenley's great-great-great-etc. grandfather in 1835 and was a study in the Greek Revival architecture popular at the time. The brick building was a long rectangle that had five steps leading up through four daunting columns to the massive oak double doors.

Tenley opened one of them for her, and Brenna blew out a breath. She could do this, she told herself, and for a second she almost believed it. Then the large oak door shut behind her and she felt all her self-doubt slide in behind her like a shadow.

Tenley smiled and waved at the guard who was sitting by the front door. Withered, probably from suffering through too many harsh New England winters, he looked old enough to have remembered the town hall being built. He adjusted his dentures before he greeted them.

"How do, Miss Tenley?" he asked.

"Doing fine, Mr. Abner, and yourself?" Tenley stopped to talk, and Brenna could feel her nerves snapping at her insides with little pinchers. She really wanted to get this over and done.

"My sciatica is acting up," he said with a grimace. "The pain shoots right down my leg just like that dang bullet I picked up in Germany in '44."

"You need to go see Doc Waters. He'll fix you up. He took care of Ruby Wolcott's pinched nerve, and she was as hunched over as a question mark," Tenley said. "Isn't that right, Brenna?"

"Huh?" Brenna asked. She was still learning the fine art of small town chitchat. No one in Boston would tell you to go to the doctor if you complained about an ache or pain. Oh, they'd tell you where to go, but it wouldn't be to the doctor.

Tenley gave her a not-so-subtle elbow to the side, and Brenna said, "Oh, yeah, Doc Waters, absolutely."

Abner narrowed his watery blue eyes at her. "You're new here."

"Yup," she said, feeling as welcome as a tick.

"That's okay. Any friend of Miss Tenley's is a friend of mine," he said. He broke into a sudden toothy smile, and Brenna suspected he shifted his dentures so much because they were too big. Maybe his gums, like the rest of him, were shrinking with age.

Either way, Brenna felt as if she had just passed the first hurdle to getting to the mayor's office.

"Maybe I'll give Doc a shout," Abner said, considering. He rolled his dentures again and then asked, "So, to what do I owe a visit from two such lovely ladies on this fine April afternoon?"

Tenley gave him a warm smile and Brenna mimicked her, but it felt unnatural, as if she were baring her teeth instead of smiling.

"We're here to see Eleanor," Tenley said.

Abner leaned back from her as if she'd said she was

bringing in the plague. "What do you want to do that for?"

"Brenna is working on a plaque for Mayor Ripley, and she thought Eleanor might like to contribute something from his office," Tenley said.

Abner glowered at the stairs to his right, and Brenna guessed there was no love lost between Abner and Ms. Sokolov.

"It's for his memorial service," Brenna said.

"Well, good luck with that," Abner grumped. "That old harpie is like a junkyard dog guarding that office. She refused to let the police in and told them they'd need a search warrant from a judge before she'd let them set foot in there. I heard Chief Barker threatened to lock her up if she didn't let his men in."

"So, did she?" Tenley asked.

"Nope," Abner said. "Chief Barker was crazy mad. I heard him say he'd be back with a warrant today, but I haven't seen him as yet."

Tenley and Brenna exchanged a wary look. It occurred to Brenna that getting past Eleanor might prove to be more difficult than dodging a pit bull with a grudge.

"Thanks for the warning, Abner," Tenley said.

"Good luck and God bless," he said. He promptly sat down at his guard's desk and assumed a pose as if he'd never seen them.

The mayor's office sat at the top of the curved staircase that climbed the wall to their right. Thirty steps up and they turned down the hallway. Dressed in his volunteer firefighter's uniform, Matt was lounging against the wall. Tenley nodded at him as she and Brenna went through another set of double doors to the right.

The temperature dropped in the large reception room

by a noticeable ten degrees. Two utilitarian chairs and a small table, with no magazines on it, filled one corner. Brenna wondered if the uninviting furniture and frigid temperature were chosen specifically to encourage people not to wait.

The burgundy carpet was squishy under her feet, and Brenna would have enjoyed the luxurious feel of it if the severe-looking woman sitting at the large rosewood receptionist's desk across the room wasn't glowering at them like they had just tracked mud on said carpet.

Brenna had no doubt that this was Eleanor Sokolov. Her half-moon reading glasses perched low on her nose and were anchored by a chain about her neck. Her eyebrows were drawn on with a pencil shades darker than the fat, sausage-sized, champagne-colored curls that rolled about her head. Brenna could picture her sleeping in cold cream and rollers every night, which would probably explain her cranky disposition. She wore a turquoise and cobalt paisley polyester blouse with a large bow at the throat. She was a stout woman, who boasted a prominent bosom that reminded Brenna of the prow of a ship.

"May I help you?" she asked, sounding as if she had no intention of doing so but good manners forbade her from saying as much.

"Hi, Ms. Sokolov," Tenley said. "It's me, Tenley M—"

"I know who you are," Ms. Sokolov interrupted. "It hasn't been that long since I caught you and your boyfriend in flagrante delicto in your car in the school parking lot. I daresay I've seen more of you than anyone should."

Tenley turned a vibrant shade of red, and Brenna felt her own eyebrows go up in surprise. Tenley caught fumbling in a car? Had it been with Matt? She could only imagine how Tenley's parents had reacted to that.

A glance at Tenley and Brenna noticed her red face had receded into blotchy patches and she was drawing in a deep breath, the kind that would precede a yell. She figured she'd better intervene before it got ugly.

"Hi," she said. "I'm Brenna Miller. I'm working on a collage for Cynthia Ripley as a memorial to the mayor, and I was wondering if you had anything you wanted to include?"

With great reluctance, Ms. Sokolov pulled her gaze away from her stare-down with Tenley. She turned to Brenna and looked her up and down, the pursing of her thin crimson lips indicating that she found her wanting. But Brenna persevered. She'd worked the art scene in Boston, dealing with snot-nosed aristocrats with more money than taste. Surely, she could handle this old broad.

"Is this the mayor's office?" she asked and strode forward.

Ms. Sokolov gaped at her as Brenna walked past. Then she leapt out from behind her desk. She was wearing a knee-length navy blue skirt that rode up higher in the back than in the front, due to her more than generous posterior. She splayed her arms across the doorway, blocking Brenna's entrance.

"You can't go in there!" she said.

"Why not?" Brenna asked. "I need more memorabilia for the collage. It'll be on display at his service, where hundreds, maybe thousands, of people will see it, and I can't have it looking shabby, now can I?"

"But this was Mr. Ripley's office," Ms. Sokolov said. "It's private."

"Hey, is that a picture of the two of you?" Brenna asked as she ducked under one of Ms. Sokolov's beefy arms and strode into the room.

Hanging on the wall, amid scores of other photos, was a small framed photo of Mayor Ripley and Ms. Sokolov, standing at a ribbon-cutting ceremony for what appeared to be the new little league fields. It was obvious from the worshipful gaze she bestowed upon him in the photo that Ms. Sokolov had more than secretarial feelings for her boss. Ew.

"That sure would be nice to add to the collage," Brenna said. "How long were you his secretary?"

"Six years," Ms. Sokolov said. She fidgeted with the large bow at her throat.

"Well, we simply have to add a photo of the two of you then, don't we? It wouldn't be right to leave you out of his memorial, now would it?"

"No, but that's the only photo I . . . we . . . have of . . ." Ms. Sokolov trailed off, obviously torn between her desire to be in the memorial and not wanting to give up perhaps the only picture of herself and her beloved boss.

"Tell you what, I'll take it to the copy store and have them run me a copy, then you can have the original back," Brenna offered.

"I suppose that would be all right," Ms. Sokolov said. "But you must be very careful with it, and now I really must ask you to leave."

Just then, on cue, Matt walked into the main office behind them.

"Excuse me, I'm here to test the fire extinguisher," he said.

"What?" Ms. Sokolov whirled around and frowned at Matt then at Tenley and then back at Matt.

"Ms. Sokolov," Matt said. "Imagine finding you here."

He walked over to the side of the room and pulled a fire extinguisher off the wall.

"Now just a minute," Ms. Sokolov protested. "These were tested six months ago. I'm sure of it. I know I have the paperwork in my file."

"New mandate," Matt said. "Testing is every six months now for municipal buildings."

"But you're just a volunteer," she protested. "Last time it was Fire Chief Levy."

"Budget cuts," Matt said. "It's tragic, but I'm willing to do my part. Oh, whoa, hey there!"

In one deft motion, he "accidentally" pulled the plastic tag, hit the lever, and dropped the hose. White foam shot across the room.

Eleanor shrieked as she was slapped across the chest by a spray of foam, which then doused her desk and a good portion of the far wall.

Matt appeared to wrestle the extinguisher to the ground. "Sorry about that," he yelled. "Good thing we tested. It must be a malfunction."

Tenley ducked her head to hide her laughter. Brenna grabbed a tissue off the desk and offered it to Ms. Sokolov, who ignored her. Eleanor had her arms raised at her sides, looking speechless, but she recovered quickly.

"Out! Out!" she yelled at Matt, looking as if she'd pick him up and throw him if he didn't move fast enough.

"Oops, uh, my bad," Matt said. He looked at the mess on the desk and took a second to appreciate Ms. Sokolov in her dither. Then he turned his back to her and winked at Tenley, who grinned back at him, before he disappeared through the door. His work here was done.

"My desk! My wall!" Ms. Sokolov cried. She swiped at the foam on her chest and hurried to her desk. She grabbed her phone and punched in numbers with shaking fingers. Then she slammed the receiver down.

"Lazy janitor," she snapped. "He's never there when I need him. I'll just have to clean it myself."

She huffed toward the door, and as soon as she rounded the doorframe, Tenley assumed the post of lookout while Brenna hurried back to search the mayor's office for information.

She began flipping through the Rolodex, past names of prominent Morse Point residents and the heads of other city departments. Nothing seemed of interest. She moved on to his desk, opening the drawers, looking for something, anything.

The top drawer was filled with pens and paperclips and a cache of wadded-up receipts. She quickly stuffed those into her pocket to examine later. After all, it wasn't as if he could get reimbursed for his expenses now.

"Brenna, hurry up," Tenley whispered. "She's in the lobby yelling at Abner. She'll be back any minute."

"Okay, okay," Brenna said. She pulled on the door to the mayor's file cabinet. It was locked. Damn.

She scanned the top of his desk. A small, round wooden box sat at one corner. It was decorated with the wrappers from different cigars. Brenna recognized it as a project Cynthia had done in decoupage class a few months ago. It seemed a likely place to keep a key.

She opened the lid and bingo. A small key sat nestled inside. Brenna snatched it up, and sure enough, it fit in the lock to the file cabinet. She flipped through the files. Some were by person's name and some were by city department. Halfway through, she spotted one that said "Morse Point Lake." Damn. She was running out of time.

She opened her black backpack purse and stuffed it inside. It really wasn't stealing if you planned to return it, right? Besides, Brenna had learned it was generally easier in life to get forgiveness than permission.

"She's halfway up the stairs," Tenley hissed.

Brenna shut and locked the cabinet, returned the key to the box, and dashed back to stand in the doorway, exactly where she'd been when Ms. Sokolov had left.

Ms. Sokolov puffed her way into the room, carrying a bucket full of cleaning supplies. Beads of sweat coated her upper lip, and one fat curl drooped over her forehead.

"You're still here," she said. She glanced between them. "You didn't touch anything, did you?"

"No, ma'am," Brenna said.

"I'll know if you did," she warned. She dumped a towel onto the floor and began to stomp on it to sop up the frothy mess. "And you can tell that Matt Collins that I'd better never see him in here again."

Tenley gave Ms. Sokolov her most withering Morse family glare. "I doubt you'll have to worry about that anytime soon."

"Humph," Ms. Sokolov dismissed them.

Together they headed for the door, Brenna feeling weak-kneed with relief that they had managed to pull it off. She could only hope that no one missed the file from the cabinet.

"Stop right there!" Ms. Sokolov's voice ordered, yanking them back like two leashed puppies.

Oh no, busted. A sick feeling of dread pooled in Brenna's belly, and she spun slowly on her heel. She could feel Tenley do the same beside her.

"You forgot this," Ms. Sokolov said. She held out the picture to Brenna.

"Oh, silly me," she said. She could feel her heart resume beating in her chest as if someone had kick-started it. "I don't know where my head is. Thank you. I'll have it back to you as soon as possible."

"I would appreciate that," Ms. Sokolov said stiffly.

"Ms. Sokolov, may I ask you a question?" Brenna asked. She knew this was foolhardy in the extreme and that she should be beating feet down the stairs and out the door, but if she didn't take this opportunity, she might not get another.

"Certainly," she said. Although, with her lips pursed tight as if pulled by a drawstring, she didn't look as if she meant it.

"Where were you the night the mayor was murdered?" she asked. She saw Tenley stiffen beside her.

Ms. Sokolov stared at Brenna with a look so cold it could have put a sheet of ice on Morse Point Lake. She did not answer. She just stared.

"Well, all right then," Brenna said, feeling awkward. "Sorry to have troubled you."

She and Tenley turned simultaneously and headed for the stairs, moving as quickly as possible without actually breaking into a run—but just barely.

# Chapter 14

Plain white glue is generally the glue of choice for decoupers, but experiment. There is a world of adhesives out there.

"Did you notice she didn't answer the question?" Brenna asked.

"I'm just surprised we weren't turned to stone back there. Yikes, she's scary," Tenley said.

They were halfway across the town green when Brenna saw Phyllis Portsmyth heading straight for them. She was wearing a pretty floral dress with pink high heels, looking as fresh as a fistful of spring flowers. She had her hand in the air, waving at them, and the midday sun sparkled off the yellow Portsmyth rock on her finger, making it almost impossible not to see her. Still, Brenna pretended she hadn't.

"Crap," she whispered. She was feeling terribly exposed and really just wanted to be back at the shop. "How are we going to avoid her?"

"No need to," Tenley said. "Follow me."

She put her chin in the air and strode forward right into Phyllis's path.

"Hello, girls," Phyllis said. "I stopped by the shop but it was all locked up."

"It's such a nice day, we decided to go for a walk," Tenley said.

"Interesting business practice," Phyllis said. The criticism was evident in her voice, but Tenley blithely ignored it.

"Prerogative of being the owner," she said.

"I suppose," Phyllis said. "You know, of course, that I won't make it to class this week. I really need to be there for Cynthia."

"I understand," Brenna said. "She's lucky to have you."

"Yes, she is. The poor thing is wracked with guilt," Phyllis said on a sigh.

Brenna felt as if everything went suddenly still. "Why would she feel guilty?"

"Oh, dear, I didn't mean . . . I really shouldn't say," Phyllis said.

"If you really don't want to," Tenley said with a shrug, "we understand."

Brenna looked at her as if she'd cracked her nut. This was information. They needed to know what she meant. Tenley gave her a quelling glance, and Brenna realized that Tenley was playing Phyllis. By pretending not to care, she was sure to get Phyllis to dish the dirt. Sheesh! Brenna was sure she would never master the subtleties of small town communication.

"Oh all right, but you have to swear not to tell anyone," Phyllis said.

"We swear," Brenna said before Tenley said something that made Phyllis change her mind.

Phyllis scouted the green and then leaned in close and continued, "You didn't hear this from me, but the night that Jim was killed, Cynthia came to my house because they'd had a terrible argument. Cynthia was hysterical. Then Nate Williams killed Jim before they could reconcile. It's just tearing Cynthia up."

Brenna sucked in a lungful of air about to proclaim Nate's innocence, but Tenley pinched her elbow.

"Ouch," she said, rubbing the spot. Tenley frowned at her and she muttered, "Darn mosquitoes."

"In April?" Phyllis asked.

"You're right," Brenna said. "It must have been a horsefly."

Phyllis gave her a curious glance and then circled around them. "I'd better be off. I promised Cynthia I'd check in on her today."

They watched as she clicked down the walkway in her narrow heels, then they turned and hurried back to Vintage Papers.

They hustled into the shop, where Matt was waiting. He was standing by the workroom table and Brenna had the feeling he'd spent his time pacing and, judging by the now empty grape bowl, eating.

"What took you so long?" he asked.

"Waylaid by Phyllis Portsmyth," she said.

"Didn't you used to date her nephew?" he asked Tenley.

There was an awkward silence, and Brenna looked back and forth between them to see who would break it first.

"Don't remind me," Tenley said, forcing a carefree air that Brenna knew she didn't feel. "He was duller than dirt. I must have been out of my mind. Needless to say, Phyllis has never forgiven me for dumping him."

Matt grinned, and Brenna couldn't tell if he was happy because Tenley called her old boyfriend dull or because she'd annoyed Phyllis or both.

"So how did it go? Did you find anything?" he asked Brenna, bringing her attention back to the task at hand.

"Pretty well, considering we had no time," she said.

"Did the old bat suspect anything?" he asked.

"No! You were fabulous," Tenley said. They gave each other a high five.

Brenna smiled at them and put the picture she'd taken from Ripley's office in the box with Cynthia's stuff. She'd have to figure out how to make that work so that Cynthia didn't notice its addition to the memorial and Ms. Sokolov did. She'd worry about that later.

"I didn't see anything in the Rolodex," she said. "But I found these receipts in his top drawer."

She emptied her pocket of the wadded-up receipts and sat down and smoothed them out on the table top.

"A restaurant in Bayview down by the Cape," she said. "It's dated a week before he died. Here's one for a gas station down there and, hmmm, a motel, too."

She exchanged a look with Tenley.

"An affair?" Tenley asked.

"Maybe," she said. "Anyone feel up to asking Cynthia about that?"

"Not me," Tenley said. "But I wonder . . ."

She fished the picture of the mayor and Ms. Sokolov out of the box and put it on the table in front of Brenna.

"Look at the way she's looking at him. She's obviously in love with him. Do you think he and Ms. Sokolov might have been doing the horizontal mambo?"

"Oh, ick," Matt groaned and clapped his hands over his eyes. "Did you have to go there? I don't want to picture that. I'm going to be scarred for life. I'm going to need therapy."

"Anyone care to ask her?" Brenna asked, smiling at Matt's dramatics.

They both shook their heads no.

"I did manage to take one other thing out of the office," Brenna said. "I got it out of his locked file cabinet. I didn't mean to take it, just look at it, but she was on her way back and it was the best clue I'd found."

She opened her backpack purse and withdrew the manila folder labeled "Morse Point Lake."

Tenley looked at it and then at her in horror.

"Would that be considered stealing evidence?" she asked.

"Not if I plan to return it," Brenna said. "It's just a temporary loan."

Matt and Tenley exchanged a look, and Brenna knew they thought she was pushing it, but how could she leave it behind when it might give them some answers?

"I promise I'll have it back before anyone knows it's missing," she said.

"Okay, then," Tenley said, still looking uncomfortable.

Truthfully, Brenna had no idea how she was going to get the folder back into the office, but she'd worry about that when the time came.

"I have to get in to work," Matt said with a regretful glance at his watch. "Let me know what you find and call me if I can help with anything else."

"Will do," Brenna said. "Thanks for everything."

"Anytime," he said.

"I'll walk you to the door," Tenley offered.

They were keeping Vintage Papers closed for the day. Tenley had called the Porter twins earlier and told them that she and Brenna were suffering from a bout of food poisoning. People generally didn't ask for many details when it was a stomach thing. They just didn't want to know.

Undoubtedly, the twins had spread the word throughout town by now. Of course, if anyone had seen them in the town hall earlier, they'd know it was a big fat lie, but that was the risk they'd had to take.

Brenna had never lived in a place where gossip moved by word of mouth faster than it did in the daily news. Truly, who needed the Internet when they lived in a town like Morse Point?

She flipped through the memos that filled the folder, scanning them for a name. She stopped when she found an architect's rendering of the townhomes and a blue print for building around the lake.

Brenna peered at the paper. She frowned. The plans included where her cabin was now. Ripley wanted to develop the entire lake. He had planned to get rid of Nate and the cabins all along.

Brenna felt a surge of fury heat her insides like a fireball. She flipped through the pages of plans, getting angrier by the moment.

Tenley came back to join her, and Brenna filled her in on what she'd discovered.

"What's that?" Tenley asked. She was pointing to a handwritten scrawl in the corner of a piece of paper.

"CRC, Cappicola Redevelopment Corporation," Brenna read. "That must be who Ripley was working with."

"I sincerely hope not," Tenley said.

"Why? Do you know them?" Brenna asked.

"Only by reputation," Tenley said. "They tried to put the squeeze on my father's firm once. They are, how do you say, well connected."

"They're mob?" Brenna gaped.

"Yep. They own most of the town of Bayview and the surrounding waterfront," Tenley said. "My father said they've been trying to extend their reach across Massachusetts for years."

"The receipts!" Brenna said. "Ripley was in Bayview just days before his death."

"So, that's why he was in such state," Tenley said. "Nate was ruining all of his plans by not selling to him, and who knows what kind of bite the Cappicolas were putting on him. These are luxury townhomes they were planning. They would have made a fortune off of these."

"This proves there is a more likely suspect," Brenna said. "We have to tell Nate."

She scooped up the folder and stuffed it back in her purse. Tenley grabbed her purse and they hurried out the front door to Brenna's Jeep. It was a quick trip out to the cabins. Brenna noticed that Tenley had a white-knuckled grip on her armrest but she said nothing, so Brenna didn't slow down. Once the cabins were in sight, it was impossible not to notice that a cluster of media cars were parked in their communal drive.

Nuts! Brenna banged her hand on the wheel. They would be mobbed by reporters if they parked anywhere near the cabins.

Tenley must have come to the same conclusion as she said, "Take your next right. We can park at the boat launch and work our way back."

Brenna passed her own drive and took a sharp right. She parked alongside the narrow gravel road that led to the boat launch and they scrambled out of the Jeep.

Tenley led the way through the woods. They had to push aside the bud-covered, whiplike branches of several forsythia bushes as they crept back toward their side of the lake. The reporters seemed to be milling around Nate's cabin, looking for any sign that he was home.

Brenna knew he had moved to the cabin beyond hers, so she and Tenley picked their way along the water's edge past her cabin to the cabin beyond. The shades were all drawn and it appeared to be deserted. She wondered how to approach it without setting Hank off in a dog explosion that would alert the reporters.

She fished in her purse until she found a peanut butter cracker. It might work.

Instead of going to the front of the cabin, where they'd be visible to the reporters, they snuck around to the back door.

"Nate," Brenna called, her voice just above a whisper. There was no answer, so she whispered his name again, this time a little louder. "Nate!"

The shade to the right of the door moved a fraction and she gave a tiny wave.

She could hear Nate talking to someone in the cabin, and she wondered if he was coaching Hank before he opened the door.

The door opened and he motioned them inside. Brenna held out the peanut butter cracker and Hank chomped it before he could get a bark out.

The cabin had the musty smell of a place that hasn't been lived in for a long while mixed with the smell of fresh paint. Tarps covered the hardwood floor in the living room, and a paint tray had a roller perched on its edge. She noticed Nate was wearing paint-splattered jeans and a faded Yankees T-shirt.

"I figured I might as well make this place rentable during my exile," he explained.

Tenley shut the door behind them and peeked out the window.

"I don't think anyone saw us," she said. They all visibly relaxed. Hank shoved his wet nose into Brenna's palm looking for another cracker.

"Can I get you both some lemonade?" Nate asked.

"Yes, please," they said in unison. The trek around the lake had made Brenna parched and she knew Tenley must feel the same.

"To what do I owe the unexpected pleasure of your company?" he asked while he poured three glasses of lemonade in the small kitchenette.

Brenna and Tenley followed him and sat at the breakfast bar that separated the kitchen and the main room.

"I had to show you what I found," Brenna said. She fished the folder out of her purse and put it on the counter.

Nate put a glass in front of each of them and took the folder in his hands. He opened it and began to leaf through the sheets of paper. He read each one, slowly and carefully, but his expression remained neutral.

Brenna sipped from her glass but her eyes never left his face. She was waiting for his reaction—surely he must be furious—but he never gave one. Not even so much as a flicker of an eyelash did he give up.

Instead, he plunked the folder onto the counter. Obviously, he wasn't getting the big picture.

"Ripley was planning to develop the lake where our houses are right now," she said.

"I see that," he said with a nod.

Tenley glanced between them. "CRC is Cappicola Redevelopment Corporation," she said. "They're mob."

"I thought that sounded familiar," Nate said. His gray gaze fastened on to Brenna. "Where did you get that folder?"

She glanced at Tenley. She was feeling uncomfortable, very much like the time she ditched school in the ninth grade and her father caught her. She glanced away from Nate's penetrating stare.

"The mayor's office," she mumbled.

"I'm sorry," he said. "I didn't catch that."

"The mayor's office," she said. "I told his secretary I needed more photos to use in the memorial Cynthia asked me to make, and I sort of took the opportunity to look around."

"And steal," he added. Brenna noticed that his nostrils flared ever so slightly when he was annoyed.

She would have protested, but a sharp rap on the front door caused them all to turn around. This time there was no stopping Hank as he propelled himself across the floor in a ferocious chorus of barks. He skidded to the door and then jumped up on his hind legs as if he'd open the door and let the person in himself.

"Nate," a deep voice called. "It's Chief Barker."

Brenna snatched the folder off the counter and stuffed it back into her purse.

She watched as Nate approached the door. Her heart was hammering in her throat. Had the chief come to see them about their visit to the town hall? Did he know she'd taken the folder? How much trouble would they be in for this? She really didn't care for the idea of a night in jail.

Nate had trouble turning the deadbolt on the front door. It would have been a fabulous stall tactic if it had been planned, but it was just that the lock was old and suffered from a lack of use.

Finally, he pulled it open. "Hi, Ray, how can I help you?"

Chief Barker entered the cabin with Officer DeFalco behind him. Neither of them looked very happy and they moved to stand in front of Nate.

"Hi, Nate." The chief ran a hand over his face. "I'm

sorry, but in light of some new evidence. I'm going to have to arrest you for the murder of Mayor Jim Ripley."

"No!" Brenna and Tenley shouted together.

"Sorry, ladies," the chief said. "I have no choice but to bring him in."

"May I ask what new evidence?" Nate asked.

Chief Barker considered him for a moment. Then he nodded. "I might as well tell you as your lawyer will find out soon enough. A witness saw your truck parked on the boat ramp on the night Ripley was killed."

"Aw, come on," Brenna protested. "He lives by the lake. Of course his truck would be parked there."

"Not on the boat ramp, it wouldn't," DeFalco said. "Not unless he was unloading something."

"Well, that's just . . ."

Nate took her hand in his and gave it a squeeze. Brenna's protest died on her lips as his silver gaze met hers in a look so intense it left her breathless. She knew he was trying to silently communicate his innocence. It was unnecessary. She nodded to let him know that she believed him. He looked relieved and the corner of his mouth turned up.

"Don't worry. I'll be all right," he said.

Officer DeFalco turned Nate around and cuffed his wrists while he read him his Miranda rights.

"Sorry, it's procedure," he said.

"No problem," Nate said. He looked back at Brenna and Tenley. "Thanks for stopping by and offering to help paint."

"Anytime," Tenley said.

"Let us know if there's anything we can do," Brenna said.

"No," Nate said, and his look was sharp. "You've done

enough. If I need *anything*, I have a lawyer who can take care of it. He's very good."

The chief glanced between them and Brenna made her face blank, not wanting to give anything away. Too late. Chief Barker came to stand in front of her and he looked less happy than he had even moments before.

He studied her carefully. "You look pale," he said. "You two should probably go see Doc Waters if your stomach bug doesn't feel better soon. I don't see how you could offer to paint a house being so sick and all."

Brenna quickly remembered their lie about the food poisoning and nodded. She didn't really have to feign being sick as she thought she might hurl from the tension right then and there.

"Oh, we're feeling much better," Brenna said. She and Tenley gave him matching fake smiles. He didn't look as if he believed them. Shocker.

"Hunh," he said and followed Nate and Officer De-Falco out the door. Silently, they watched the hovering reporters mob Nate as he was folded into the back of a waiting cruiser.

"That was close," Tenley said as she sank back down into her seat. "It sounds like Nate wants us to drop it."

"I think he's worried," Brenna agreed.

"About?" Tenley asked.

"Whoever killed the mayor coming after us," she said.

"Oh, that would be bad," Tenley agreed.

"Not as bad as an innocent man going to jail for a crime he didn't commit," Brenna said.

"You've got that look on your face again," Tenley said and shook her head. "What are you going to do?"

"Nothing," Brenna said. "But I do I think it's time for a road trip."

"Bayview?" Tenley asked, and Brenna nodded. "Excellent. I could use some fried clams. I call shotgun."

"No," Brenna said. "I don't want you involved any more than you already are."

"Sweetie, I'm your best friend, I'm already involved up to my ears," Tenley said. "Besides, if you don't let me come with you, I'll go to the jail and tell Nate what you're up to."

"You wouldn't," she said.

"Try me," Tenley said. Her chin was tilted up in full Morse stubborn mode.

"Oh, fine," Brenna said. She tried to sound put out, but truthfully she was relieved. It was always nice to have backup, just in case.

As soon as they had jotted down the pertinent names and addresses and plotted their course on a map, they set out in Brenna's Jeep. The drive to Bayview took two bags of Chili Cheese Fritos, two Dr Pepper Big Gulps, and a shared package of Hostess Snowballs, the pink ones. It also took two hours with one bathroom break to slog their way through the rush hour traffic that congested the highway like a particularly nasty head cold.

Bayview was a tourist Mecca that sat at the heel of Cape Cod. Filled with beachfront inns, bed-and-breakfasts, hotels, and motels, it was the crossing point for all traffic headed out to the Cape on Route 6. It was also a thoroughfare for the travelers catching the ferry to Martha's Vineyard from Woods Hole, making it the center of all traffic flow.

They decided on the drive to stop at the restaurant that the mayor had eaten at first and see if anyone remembered him. It was called Vincent's.

Brenna got off the main road and took the shoreline drive that Tenley pointed out. As the sun set, they passed a large marsh on one side and a housing development on the other. As they broke through the trees, the road turned and the marshland gave way to ocean with small businesses lining the opposite side of the narrow road. Within three miles, Vincent's came into view. It was a large, gray brick building that boasted a view of the water on three sides through its floor-to-ceiling windows.

It was six o'clock, the height of the dinner hour, and Brenna and Tenley found themselves tenth in line, waiting to speak with the hostess. During a quick scan of the room, Brenna noticed that most of the people in the restaurant were older. The décor was bland, everything in shades of mauve and gray, as if the restaurant didn't want to compete with its majestic view of the ocean.

When they were second in line, Brenna heard Tenley gasp and she turned to see what was wrong.

Tenley was staring open-mouthed at a large portrait that hung on the wall behind the hostess. Brenna studied the four foot by six foot painting of a man with an impressive schnozz and a Sinatra-esque smile, but she couldn't find anything alarming about it.

"What is it?" she asked.

Tenley leaned close and whispered, "That portrait."

"Yeah, what about it?"

"That's Vincent . . . Vincent Cappicola," Tenley hissed.

"He owns the restaurant?"

"So it would seem."

"What should we do?"

"Hi, can I help you?" the hostess asked them.

Brenna didn't see that there was much they could do at

this juncture. They had to find out whom the mayor had met here even if it was the owner himself.

"Hi," she said. She fumbled in her purse for the photo of Mayor Ripley that she'd taken from the box Cynthia had given her. "I was wondering if you remember seeing this man here, last Thursday?"

The hostess glanced over Brenna's shoulder at the waiting line.

"We're kind of busy, lady, are you planning on eating here or not?"

Brenna handed her a twenty. "Does it matter?"

"I suppose not," the hostess said as she pocketed the money. She had cranberry red hair, styled in a severe bob, and she kept a pencil behind her right ear. The name embroidered in navy blue on her pale blue polo shirt was Dottie. She frowned at the picture Brenna held out to her, then her face cleared. "Yeah, I remember him. He was a total pain in the ass."

"How so?" Tenley asked. Her eyes were darting around the restaurant as if she expected the Cappicolas to come out with guns blazing at any moment.

"No table was good enough for him," Dottie said. "I had to move him four times. He kept saying how he was friends with the owner and he was going to report me if I didn't give him good enough service. What a jerk."

"Was he friends with the owner?" Brenna asked.

"Given that the owner is my Uncle Vinnie," she said and pointed her thumb at the portrait behind her, "and the fact that I'd never seen the jerk before, I'd have to say no."

"Is your uncle in tonight?" Tenley asked.

"No," Dottie said. "He's retired. My cousin Dom oversees the family business now."

"Is Dom here?"

"No, he's out on business. He won't be back until tomorrow."

"One more question, Dottie," Brenna said. "If you don't mind?"

"Not a bit," she said. She wiggled her fingers under Brenna's nose. Brenna sighed and put another twenty in the girl's hand.

"Was the jerk with anyone?" she asked.

Dottie closed her eyes as if trying to remember. "Yeah, he had a date. A skinny little blond lady, dressed nice, lots of diamonds, but still looked like there were lots of miles on her tires, you know what I'm saying?"

"Cynthia," Brenna and Tenley said together.

"Thanks, Dottie," Brenna said. "You've been a big help."

"Anytime," Dottie said. "Now can I show you two to a table?"

Brenna glanced at the portrait of Vincent looming over them. "Not tonight but thanks."

Dottie shrugged, looked past her, and barked, "Next!"

They left the restaurant quickly. Neither of them spoke until they were back out in the salty sea air.

"Retired?" Tenley asked. "Can you retire from the mob?"

"I don't know. I thought the retirement package came with monogrammed cement anklets," Brenna said.

"I need comfort food," Tenley said. Her voice held just the barest hint of a whimper.

"Me, too," said Brenna. "Let's go."


The lobster roll was perfect. The toasted split-top roll, the kind only found in New England, was grilled on the sides and stuffed to bursting with lobster meat drenched in butter. The butter ran down her fingers while Brenna tried to savor each bite, but it was still gone too soon.

She and Tenley had found a drive-in seafood restaurant called Chick's a few miles up the shoreline from Vincent's. They parked along the water's edge and sat on the hood of the Jeep. With a take-out container full of clam strips and French fries between them, they munched in silence as they watched the waves roll in.

"Do you think the Cappicolas offed Ripley?" Tenley asked.

"I don't know," Brenna answered. She'd been mulling over the same thing. "It appears that he and Cynthia came down here. Maybe it was just a day trip. Maybe it had nothing to do with Morse Point Lake being developed."

"Maybe, but it seems unlikely," Tenley said. "Why would he have the Cappicolas' name scribbled in his file and why would he be eating at their restaurant if he wasn't trying to court their business?"

"Those are some pretty dangerous people to go into business with," Brenna said.

"Maybe he couldn't he find anyone else," Tenley said.

"Or maybe he needed someone who was more powerful than Nate," Brenna said. "Maybe the Cappicolas were the only people who had the clout he needed."

"Yikes," Tenley said.

"Agreed."

"Shall we go and check out the motel?" Tenley asked. She wadded up her wrappers and bagged the empty boxes. She dumped them in a nearby garbage can.

"Might as well," Brenna said. "I wish we could find some evidence that Ripley met with Dottie's cousin Dom, however. I get the feeling there was something she wasn't telling us, and right now it all seems so flimsy."

"Very circumstantial," Tenley agreed.

They climbed back into the Jeep and followed the directions to the Red Pony Inn. It was several miles away, and now that it was completely dark, Brenna was forced to drive more slowly along the unfamiliar road.

She wasn't sure when she started to get the hinky feeling that they were being followed, but given that the stretch of road they were on was becoming increasingly desolate, she found it odd that the large sedan behind them was maintaining a precise distance between them.

"Tenley," she said. "I'm going to pull over up ahead. Could you get the license plate of the car behind us when it passes?"

"Problem?" Tenley asked.

"Not yet," Brenna said. "I may just be paranoid, but I can't help feeling like we've picked up a tail."

"A Buick of a tail, no less," Tenley said as she glanced behind them. She fished in her purse for a piece of paper and a pen. "Okay, I'm ready."

Brenna quickly cut the wheel to the right, hoping to catch the Buick by surprise. She did. It sailed passed them as Tenley quickly jotted down the plate number illuminated in the Jeep's headlights.

"Got it," she said.

"Good, because it looks as if they're turning around."

"What?" Tenley cried as she glanced up from the paper in her hand. "Geez, I really thought you were just being twitchy."

Brenna didn't wait for the Buick to complete its K turn on the narrow road. She stomped on the gas, while the Buick floundered like a compass needle seeking north, and sped around its back end.

Tenley turned around in her seat to keep an eye on the Buick. "They're reversing now."

Brenna kept her eyes on the road in front of her. Several neon signs reading VACANCY whipped by; still she pressed on.

"They're back on the road. They're closing the gap between us." Tenley's voice rose higher in pitch with her increasing panic.

Ahead, Brenna saw the Red Pony Inn. She knew she couldn't outrun the Buick on unfamiliar terrain. She could feel her insides crackle with anxiety. She had a split second to make her decision and hope it was the right one.

Again, she yanked the wheel sharply to the right. Tenley fell half into her seat and then jolted forward as Brenna slammed on the brakes in front of the motel office.

The Buick bounced into the parking lot behind them.

"Come on," Brenna yelled. "Let's go."

They dashed out of the Jeep and sprinted through the front door of the office. Brenna pulled it closed behind them and swiftly turned the dead bolt.

"Can I help you?" The night clerk peered over the counter at them. He was holding a Marvel comic book in one hand and a red Mountain Dew in the other.

"Oh no!" Tenley grabbed Brenna's hand and pointed at the far wall.

Brenna looked and felt her mouth slide open. The same portrait that had been in Vincent's restaurant hung on the wall in front of them.

Just then a key turned in the lock on the front door. Tenley let out a strangled cry and they clutched each other close as whoever had been following them in the Buick was about to enter the inn.

# Chapter 15

Dip the cutout in a bowl of water until the paper is saturated so it will take the adhesive more easily.

A man wearing a navy blue suit, impeccably cut to fit his trim but muscled body, entered the inn with two gentlemen, also in dark suits, behind him.

"Good evening, Mr. Cappicola," the night clerk greeted him. Brenna noticed that he swiftly hid the soda and the magazine under the counter. "How are you tonight?"

Brenna felt Tenley tremble beside her. Obviously, they had found Dom Cappicola, or rather he had found them.

"Fine, Jason, just fine," the man said.

His gaze swept over Brenna and Tenley. His head tilted to the side as if they weren't what he had been expecting. With his chiseled features complemented by dark eyes and hair, he was undeniably handsome. But Brenna had met a lot of handsome men in her life, and none of them had exuded raw power like Dom Cappicola.

He crossed the room and stopped in front of her, and she felt extremely self-conscious, overly aware of her unruly windblown hair, her lack of makeup, her grubby jeans, and navy blue hoodie. She would have felt so much better if she were wearing the female equivalent of his power suit. Say, her black rope dress from Tahari. Yes, that would have made her feel much less like a wayward adolescent under his scrutinizing glance.

Brenna looked from him to the portrait on the wall and then back at him. Meanwhile, Tenley was making small whimpering noises in her throat.

"You look younger than your portrait, Mr. Cappicola," she said.

His mouth twitched as if he was amused. "I should hope so," he said. "That's my father."

She could see it then, the family resemblance. He had the same schnozz as his father, but it didn't overpower his face like it did his father's. This younger Cappicola had a strong square jaw, which balanced his nose. And now that he was standing closer, she noticed his eyes were a warm shade of chocolate brown, not the coal black of the man in the portrait.

"My name is Dom," he said. "Dominick Cappicola."

He held out his hand and Brenna shook it. Her fingers were icy from the chilly evening air and from sheer terror, but if he noticed, he said nothing.

"Brenna Miller," she said. "And this is my friend Tenley Morse."

Generations of good breeding forced Tenley to unclamp herself from Brenna's side and shake his hand.

"These are my associates Paulie and Sal," Dom said. "Now that we've all met, I was wondering if you ladies would give me the pleasure of your company in the diner over there. I have some questions for you."

"Oh, we'd love to, really," Brenna said. "But . . .

"We've got a sick cat . . . er . . . aunt," Tenley stammered.

"At home," Brenna finished. "And we need to get back immediately."

"I'm sorry to hear about your aunt . . . er . . . cat," Dom said with a sympathetic nod and just a trace of mockery. "But this isn't a request. Shall we?"

Paulie or Sal, Brenna was unclear as to which was who, opened the door for them and they filed back out into the brisk evening air.

The diner was across the parking lot from the inn. It was a stand-alone steel and glass building that had an oily aroma about it as if it existed in its own personal grease bubble. With every step closer, Brenna was sure they were inching nearer to their doom.

What if Dom had murdered Mayor Ripley? What if he thought they knew and had proof? Was he going to stuff them into trunks and float them, too? She wanted to grab Tenley's hand, break into a run, and escape, but she doubted they'd make it to the edge of the parking lot.

One of his two goons opened the door, and Dom gestured to them to go first. Brenna walked in with Tenley behind her. She glanced around the tiny, red vinyl and chrome room and was disturbed to find that it was empty, save a waitress, who was sitting at the counter, chewing a wad of gum, and reading the latest issue of *US* magazine.

Brenna saw Dom turn to talk to Sal and Paulie. They nodded. She watched through the window as the taller of the two leaned against the side of the building and lit a cigarette. The other one disappeared around the back of the building, as if he had been sent to watch the rear door.

Tenley gave her an alarmed look, and Brenna knew that she had seen him, too.

"Have a seat," Dom said. He looked at the waitress and barked, "Three coffees, Gina. Please."

Brenna and Tenley squeezed into a booth in front of the window. Maybe if someone drove by and saw them, they'd be rescued. Brenna decided to cling to that life raft. The waitress slid off the stool, looking put out. Brenna thought that took some nerve, considering who her boss was.

"Now Brenna, Tenley, let's get acquainted, shall we?" he asked.

Gina plunked three steaming cups of coffee and a bowl of creamers in front of them.

"Thank you," Brenna said. She tried to make eye contact with the young woman to let her know they were in trouble, but Gina didn't even glance at her.

She stirred in two sugars and two creamers, but the black sludge was as thick as melted tire rubber and seemed to absorb the creamers, remaining the same black shade as before.

Dom looked at his with equal disgust. "Sorry, I bet this is left over from this morning." He pushed his cup away with a sigh.

"Is there something we can help you with?" Brenna asked. Her nerves were close to the breaking point. If Dom had an issue with them, she wanted to know about it.

"You came to Vincent's," he said. His gaze moved from her to Tenley, where it lingered.

"That's right," Tenley said. She shook her long blond hair and Dom looked entranced. Brenna rolled her eyes. Men had been having this reaction to Tenley since they were in college. She'd feel sorry for them, but really, Tenley was such a nice person, they'd be lucky to have her.

"So?" Brenna asked, trying to get on with the discussion.

Dom shook his head. "So . . . er . . . well, Dottie is my cousin, and she told me you were asking questions about Jim Ripley."

"That's right," Brenna said.

"Why?" he asked.

Again, she felt that surge of power emanate from him, and she knew this was not a man to cross. What should she tell him? Somehow accusing him of murder seemed a bad way to go. She went for a version of the truth instead.

"Ripley was murdered," she said.

He tilted his head, considering her. She noticed he didn't look surprised by the news.

"I heard about that," he confirmed. "Why does that bring you here?"

"A friend of ours has been wrongly arrested for the murder. We need to find out what really happened to Jim Ripley."

"So naturally, you came to Bayview to accuse the Cappicolas," Dom said. He looked annoyed.

Brenna met his dark gaze and knew that if Dom had killed Ripley, they wouldn't be leaving Bayview, at least not the way they had come. She had nothing to lose.

"We found Ripley's receipts from Vincent's and the Red Pony Inn dated a week before he died," she said. Tenley gasped beside her, but Brenna forged on. "We have to find out what he was doing down here. Look, we're not accusing anyone, we're just trying to help our friend."

Dom studied Brenna. His look was admiring. "He's a lucky man."

"Who?" she asked.

"The man who generates so much loyalty from two such lovely ladies," he said.

This time his eyes stayed on Brenna's face, and she felt her cheeks grow warm with embarrassment. Good grief, was he flirting with her?

"Did you talk to Ripley?" she asked. She made her voice crisp and businesslike. A small smile played on his lips and she got the feeling she didn't fool him one bit.

"I did," he said.

Brenna and Tenley both gasped. This could be it. The information they needed.

"He wanted Cappicola Redevelopment Corporation to invest in a project in Morse Point," he said. "He proposed building townhomes around a lake up there."

"And?" Brenna asked.

"And I said no," Dom said.

"What about your father?" Brenna asked. "Did he say no?"

"My father is retired," Dom said. "He hasn't run any aspect of the family business in over a year."

It was quiet at their small table.

"Why did you say no?" Brenna asked.

Dom glanced between the two of them, as if trying to decide whether they were trustworthy or not. Finally, he leaned over the table and motioned them closer. They leaned in.

"There was too much heat from that artist guy up there," he said. "It was not a sound investment. Ripley had some big ideas of me sending some of my guys up there to muscle him out, but . . ."

"But what?" Brenna prompted him.

He lifted his hand and tapped his fist against his lips, again considering them. He lowered his arm and leaned forward once again.

"I'm sure you know my family's reputation."

"Well connected," Tenley said.

"Mobbed up," Brenna added.

"Hoodlums," Tenley volleyed.

"Gangstas," Brenna countered.

"Yes, yes, thank you," Dom said. He looked a little irked and they both went quiet. "Well, the thing is, I'm trying to make the family business legit."

Brenna and Tenley both sat back, flabbergasted. They couldn't have been more surprised if he'd said he was really a woman.

"Really?" Tenley asked. "But the Cappicolas have been connected for as long as I can remember."

"I know," Dom said. "I've been getting some static from the family, but I went to Harvard, for Pete's sake. I can't be mob."

Why this struck Brenna as funny, she had no idea. Perhaps it was the relief that she would not be floating in a box at the end of the evening after all. Either way, she felt a snort escape her and then another. The harder she tried to stop it, the harder she laughed. Tenley must have felt the same relief because she started laughing, too.

Annoyed by the noise, the waitress hopped off her stool with a huff and took her magazine to the back.

Dom gave them a rueful grin and said, "You remember my two friends?"

They nodded.

"Well, Paulie went to MIT and Sal went to Harvard with me and graduated magna cum laude. He's actually a CPA."

Brenna broke into a fresh peal of laughter and Tenley joined her. They'd been terrorized by an Ivy League accountant.

"So, how did the mayor react when you told him you

were going legit?" Brenna asked, once she'd stopped laughing.

"I didn't tell him," Dom said. "I have a reputation to maintain and I'd appreciate it if you didn't mention it to anyone either."

"Our lips are sealed," Brenna promised. "So what did you tell Ripley?"

"I just told him no," he said. "I told him it was bad business to try and oust a renowned artist, who appeared to be willing to come out of seclusion to fight him. I told him he should come up with a new location."

"How'd he take that?" Tenley asked.

"He was pretty steamed," Dom said. "And the blond he was with didn't look too happy either."

"His wife, Cynthia," Brenna said. "She's the force behind the man."

"I'll say," Dom said. "When I left their table, they were hissing at each other like a pair of snakes. Scary."

"We can imagine," Brenna said.

"Besides, even if the townhomes were a good deal, I would have passed. I don't want any more investments in Morse Point," Dom said. "I'm trying to diversify."

"You have investments in Morse Point?" Brenna asked.

"Just one," Dom said. "And it's not a moneymaker. In fact, we're thinking of cutting it loose."

"What is it?" Tenley asked.

"Cappicola Industries owns the *Morse Point Courier* as well as three other town papers in that area," he said. "The *Courier* is lagging. If it can't manage to sell more papers, we're going to have to shut it down."

Brenna felt herself get a touch light-headed. It was all coming into focus now. Ed Johnson's paper was owned by the Cappicolas, and if he didn't up the sales, he was going

out of business. He needed a big story, and boy, did he ever get one. Interesting.

A glance at her watch showed it was getting late. Now that she had some information of value, she couldn't wait to get back to Morse Point to tell Nate.

With a none too gentle shove, she pushed Tenley out of the booth. "Look at the time."

Tenley gave her a curious glance but followed her lead by giving a big yawn.

"Well, it was nice to meet you, Dom," Brenna said as she stood beside the booth. "Er . . . thanks for the coffee."

He rose and stood in front of her, blocking her path to the exit. For a fleeting second, she wondered if he was going to stop them from leaving. Then he smiled and she shook her head. Probably, that aura of power he put off was genetic like his hair and eye color. He just couldn't help it.

He took her hand in his and pressed a business card into her palm. His hand was large and warm where it enveloped hers, and Brenna felt her pulse skitter at the contact.

"If you have any more questions, call me."

"Okay," she said. Her voice cracked and she cleared her throat. She pulled her hand out of his, feeling like an idiot.

As she made her way home, Brenna watched Bayview disappear in her rearview mirror with the realization that sometimes people just plain surprised you, for better and for worse.


It was late when Brenna dropped off Tenley at her house and then headed out to her cabin. The beams from her head-

lights bounced as the Jeep bobbed along the quiet road, which was jutted with potholes, remnants from several merciless New England winters.

She was tired from the inside out, and the only thing she wanted to see for the next eight hours was the inside of her eyelids. She wouldn't, of course, because as soon as it opened, she planned to be at the jail, telling Nate what she'd found out about Dom Cappicola and Mayor Ripley.

She climbed from her car, grateful to find no reporters waiting in the communal parking lot. She stepped briskly toward her cabin, glancing over her shoulder as she unlocked the door and let herself in.

The cabin was dark. Normally, she left a light on when she knew she was going to be out late, but she'd had no idea when she woke up this morning that the day would include Nate's arrest and a road trip to the Cape.

She fumbled for the light switch, but before she could reach it, the standing lamp in the corner flicked on. Brenna screamed and a rush of adrenaline hit her like the zap of a long-fingered lightning bolt. She jumped into her fighter stance, ready to kick some serious tail if necessary.

"Whoa." Nate raised his hands as if in surrender. He was sitting in the corner chair between the lamp and the bookcase, and judging by the look of his puffy eyes, he'd been asleep when she came in.

"Are you nuts?" she yelled. She put her hand over her racing heart. "You scared me to death. What if I had pepper-sprayed you?"

"Then I imagine we'd both be runny-eyed and sneezing right now," he said. He stood and crossed the room toward her. "I'm sorry. I didn't mean to startle you."

"It's f—fine," she stammered. But it wasn't. She felt

sickly and faint, her skin was clammy, and her teeth were chattering.

"Are you okay?" he asked. All traces of sleep were gone as his gray eyes bored into hers, and he grabbed her elbow and helped her to the nearest seat.

She dropped her head between her knees. Nate crouched down beside her so he could see her face.

"Is this because of what happened to you in Boston?" he asked.

# Chapter 16

Smooth the paper onto the surface with damp fingers so they won't stick to the paper.

Brenna tilted her face up and found him just inches in front of her. She put her head back down. Truly, hadn't this day been long enough?

"What makes you think anything happened in Boston?" she asked.

"You have safety issues," he said. "I assumed they came from your time in Boston."

"I'm just cautious-natured," she said.

"Uh-huh," he said.

He sounded dubious, but he didn't press and she was grateful. She didn't think she was going to pass out anymore, so she slowly raised her head and rested it on her folded arms on her knees.

"Can you eat?" he asked. "You look like you could probably use some food."

It had been hours since the lobster roll at the shore. She nodded.

"Follow me," he said.

He stood and led the way into the kitchen. While she sat at the counter, he raided her refrigerator for eggs, milk, cheese, and salsa.

She marveled that he was here, in her kitchen, doing something as domestic as cooking when he should be in jail.

"How did you get out of jail?" she asked.

"I told you, it's all who you know," he said. "Well, that and a heavy chunk of my savings used as bail."

"So, who do you know?"

"An art collector judge, a badger of a defense attorney, and a chief of police who really didn't want to arrest me anyway."

"It *is* all who you know," she said. With sudden clarity she realized that, as reclusive as he was, Nate moved in elevated circles of circumstance that she would never know.

She watched as he cooked the beaten eggs on the bottom of the pan, layered sharp cheddar cheese on top, and then gently folded the eggs around the cheese into the shape of a half moon. When he turned the omelet onto a plate, he put spoonfuls of salsa and sour cream on top, handed Brenna a fork, and said, "Eat."

"I didn't know you could cook," she said. The eggs smelled delicious and she tucked into them with gusto.

"How do you think I feed myself?" he asked.

"I thought you were living off my baking efforts," she said. He laughed and she liked the way his eyes crinkled in the corners. He made an omelet for himself and then sat down beside her.

"So, are you going to answer my question?" he asked.

She sighed. "I had a feeling you hadn't forgotten."

"Not that I'm badgering or anything," he said.

"Aren't you more interested in what Tenley and I found out tonight?" she asked.

"If that's what you want to talk about," he said. "But I have to ask, do you get panic attacks a lot?"

"That was not a panic attack," she corrected him. "That was a borderline hysteric reaction to finding someone in my house when no one was supposed to be there."

"Point taken. Sorry," he said and hung his head, looking much like Hank when he was being chastised.

"It's okay," she said. "How did you get in, by the way?"

"Master key. As soon as I was released, I called Matt. I'm glad you and Tenley had the good sense to let him know where you were going. I waited in my cabin as long as I could stand it." Nate's voice was low when he added, "But I got worried and came over here."

He sounded genuinely anxious on her behalf, and Brenna had no idea what to make of that. She did know that the thought of him having a key to her place didn't bother her as much as it should.

"Sorry you were worried. We were fine, although we didn't know it," she said. She hesitated, not wanting to divulge what Dom had asked her to keep quiet, but then decided Nate would respect her confidence and not blab. "Please keep this between you and me. It turns out young Mr. Cappicola is a Harvard grad, trying to turn the family business legit."

Nate put his fork down and stared at her. "No way."

"Way," she said. "Ripley approached him about the lake proposal, but Dom declined. He didn't like the potentially problematic aspect of throwing you out."

"*Dom*, is it?" he asked. He raised his eyebrows questioningly and Brenna was mortified to feel her face grow warm.

"He was very nice," she said.

"I'm sure he was," he said.

"It gets better," she said in an effort to get the conversation back on track.

"What, do you have a date with him?" he asked. He sounded a bit miffed. Brenna stifled the urge to roll her eyes.

"No," she said. "I have even better information."

Nate jabbed his fork into his eggs with a little more force than necessary. Brenna decided to ignore this.

"Guess who owns the *Morse Point Courier*?" she asked.

"No idea," he said.

"Cappicola Industries," she said.

"You're kidding?" he asked. His gaze met hers and she raised her hands in exasperation.

"Do I look like I'm kidding?" she asked. She was feeling pretty proud of herself and her detective work. "And that's not all."

"Of course not," he said. He pushed his plate away and looked as if he was bracing himself for her next bit of news. "What else did you find out?"

"That if Ed Johnson doesn't start selling more newspapers, he's going to be shut down."

"*Dom* told you that?" he asked.

"Yes," she said.

"And you believed him?" he asked. He didn't even try to hide the skepticism in his voice.

"Of course," she said. "Why would he lie?"

"Oh, I don't know," he said. "Let's see, maybe to throw suspicion off of himself and onto Ed?"

"That's ridiculous," she said. "If you had met him, you'd see."

"Well, I won't be meeting him," Nate said. "That is Chief Barker's job, not mine or yours."

"But . . ."

"No buts," he said. "I want you to leave this alone. The police can investigate Ripley's murder. That's what we pay them to do."

"The police make mistakes," she said with her teeth clenched. Sometimes, despite her best efforts, the bitterness of her past got the better of her. Nate opened his mouth to speak but she pressed on, "I think if I can get into Ed's office . . ."

"No, absolutely not," he said.

"Why not?" She stood up and carried her empty plate to the sink. "It's no different than visiting Ripley's office."

"Yet another thing I didn't want you to do," he said. He followed her to the sink, put his plate on top of hers, and turned to face her. "There's no memorial to decoupage here. You'd be straight up breaking and entering. And having been arrested for just a few hours today, I highly recommend avoiding a stay in the local jail."

"I'm not going to get arrested," she said. "All I'm going to do is search Ed's office to see if there is anything that links him to the mayor's murder."

"Like what?" Nate asked. "The key to the trunk?"

"Don't be silly, he wouldn't keep that lying around," she said.

"That was sarcasm." He ran a hand through his brown wavy hair. She noticed he did that when he was feeling particularly exasperated.

"Look, they let you out, because of who you are, and because you can pay an inordinate amount of bail," she said. "But do you really think they won't come after you again, if they don't find out who really did it?"

"So what?" he asked.

"So? Everyone will think you're a murderer. People will whisper behind your back and point at you."

"And that would be different how?" he asked. He had a point. He wasn't the friendliest sort and the locals had been whispering about him even before the mayor's murder.

"Trust me," she said. "When people believe the worst of you, it cuts deep."

She turned away from him and walked back to the brown suede couch that ran along one wall of her living room. She sank down into it and he sat down beside her. His eyes were intent as they studied her face.

"Tell me what happened to you," he said.

Brenna studied him. His eyes were patient and, to her undoing, full of empathy. She swallowed hard. She never spoke of the events that had led to her move to Morse Point. They were still quite painful, but she had a feeling Nate would understand. She hoped so at any rate.

"Two years ago, I was closing the gallery by myself. We'd just received the crates for our next event, an auction of Jean Depaul's turn-of-the-century works, and I was charged with doing the inventory before I left."

Brenna paused. The memories of being in the gallery that night filled her mind. She'd been nibbling on Havarti cheese and wheat crackers and listening to Mozart on the stereo. She had always loved the cavernous gallery at night and was happy to do inventory. She'd felt it was a treat to get to be the one to open the crates and see the works first.

She'd opened half of the crates when she got that creepy feeling of another presence in the gallery. At first, she thought it was one of the gallery owners stopping by to take a peek at Depaul's work, but when she called out, no one answered. She told Nate about that feeling and he nodded.

"I knew something was wrong," she said. "So I decided to get out of there. I wanted to call the police but my cell phone was in my purse in the back and I didn't want to go back there. In the main room, I felt safer, as if someone on the street might see me, so I made my way toward the front door."

She paused to take a long breath. Even two years later, this part bothered her.

"I was halfway to the door when I was attacked," she said. "To this day I am not sure where they came from. I was knocked down, and when I tried to put up a fight, they took one of the small sculptures we had on display and cracked me on the temple with it."

She lifted back her hair and showed him the small scar at her hairline.

"Ouch," he winced. "What happened?"

"They stole every single piece of Jean Depaul's work," Brenna said. "And I was left in a pool of blood and wasn't found until the next morning when the owners arrived to open the gallery."

"You could have died," he said. His voice was tight with anger and somehow that made Brenna feel better.

"There were days that I would have preferred that ending," she said. He frowned. "The police fingered me for the robbery."

"What? But that's ridiculous," he said.

"The burglars had done their homework," she said. "They stole my identity and started offering the works on the black market using my name. No one believed me. Not the police, not my bosses, not my clients. My reputation in the art world was destroyed."

# Chapter 17

A brayer is a hand roller used in decoupage to help remove wrinkles and excess glue.

Nate let out a hiss of pent-up breath. "Good God, Brenna, I am so sorry. I remember hearing about that robbery."

She nodded. She could feel a lump in her throat and tears sting her eyelids. She blinked them away and swallowed, forcing the knot down.

"It's okay," she said, although it wasn't and it never would be. "They finally caught the thief and I was proven innocent, but the damage done to my reputation was irreparable."

Nate put his hand over hers. His palm was warm against the chill that engulfed her.

"So that's why you didn't want your name in the paper when you discovered the mayor's body," he said.

"Yeah, I've seen my name in print enough to last a lifetime," she said. "My parents were appalled. Millers are only supposed to be listed in the society pages, not the police blotter."

She glanced at him and saw his frown deepen.

"But you were a victim," he said. "I mean, you could have been killed."

"Hmm," she said.

There was no way she could explain. Her mother had spent her entire life cultivating her reputation as the perfect high-society wife and mother. To have her daughter fingered as a felon, even mistakenly, was too much for her to bear, no matter how innocent Brenna had been.

Her mother had yet to forgive her for embarrassing them by being attacked, and if that weren't bad enough, Brenna had taken the witness stand and sent the real thief to prison, giving her mother even more to be embarrassed about.

"I didn't do very well after the robbery," she said. "I couldn't function. I was afraid of my own shadow, and everyone else's for that matter. It was devastating."

He squeezed her hand in an almost painful grip that she welcomed. The pain brought her back to the present. She pulled her hand out of his and pushed a stray lock of hair off her face.

"Of course, it got worse before it got better. I spent my days coming up with reasons why I couldn't leave my apartment. I had lost my job at the gallery after the burglary and then my boyfriend James dumped me."

Nate looked empathetic, as if he understood. She appreciated that, but of course he couldn't understand what it had been like between her and James after the robbery. She hadn't been much of a girlfriend. She hadn't been much of anything.

"I knew I needed to get out of Boston," she said. "So, when Tenley called and told me about her shop and that she was looking for help, I jumped at the chance."

"I'm glad," he said.

His gaze was warm, and again Brenna wasn't quite sure what he meant, but it felt good nonetheless.

"Now, the reason I told you all this was twofold. One, you can't just leave things to the police. They make mistakes. I mean, they actually believed I'd lie in my own blood all night and then use my own name to market stolen pieces of art. Ridiculous. And reason two is to show that I can handle it," she said. "I'm not a fragile little flower."

"No, never that," Nate said dryly.

"Is that sarcasm?" she asked.

"You think?" he retorted.

"Listen," she said. "I'm going to the *Courier*'s offices, and I'm going to see what I can find, because I like Morse Point, and although it's taken me a year, I feel like I belong here and I don't want to leave."

"Why would you leave?" he asked.

"Because I can't live in a town with an unsolved murder," she said. "I'll become all paranoid again and have to move."

"The murder isn't going to go unsolved," Nate said. "Chief Barker will figure it out."

"By arresting you?" she asked.

"I'm a natural suspect, given the very public disagreements the mayor and I shared," Nate said.

"Yeah, just like the Boston PD tried to make me out to be the art thief," she said. "They actually tried to make people believe that I gave myself a concussion to make myself look innocent. They never considered that maybe I was innocent."

"This isn't Boston," he said. He tilted his head as he studied her and his eyes were kind. But Brenna was too full of the demons from her past to let it go.

"What's your point?" she countered. She crossed her arms over her chest and sank deeper into the cushy suede of her couch.

"That whoever floated the mayor did me a favor," he said.

She gave him a wide-eyed look.

"Oh, not like that," he said. "I am sorry the mayor is dead, but whoever dumped him, thinking to pin me, made me look more innocent than guilty. Ray can't believe I'd be that dumb and neither can the judge. So you see? You need to stop."

"Stop what?" she asked.

"Stop investigating," he said. "Don't search the newspaper office or anyplace else that might put you in harm's way."

Brenna opened her mouth to protest, but he put up his hand to stop her.

"Promise," he said.

She sighed. "I promise not to put myself in harm's way," she said. There. That was nice and loosely stated.

His gaze was fierce. "There is a murderer out there, Brenna, someone who had no problem bashing the mayor's head in, stuffing him in a trunk, and tossing him into the lake. Now what do you think he'd do to you if you find him before the chief does?"

"All right, all right," she said grudgingly.

Nate sat back into the couch, relieved. It was nice that he cared, Brenna thought, but he didn't understand. She was positive if the chief didn't find the real murderer and soon, Nate would find himself heading right back to jail, only next time he might not get out.

Brenna knew what it was like to be wrongly accused.

She didn't want to watch Nate go through that, and she simply couldn't live in a town where a murderer roamed free.

It wasn't that she was disregarding her promise to Nate, Brenna told herself. It was just that a girl had to run errands and if, in the course of those errands, polite conversation included the murder, well, that couldn't be helped.

Brenna decided to stop by Stan's Diner to see who was out and about. She hadn't had the chance to chat up Marybeth DeFalco, and she knew from the way the Porter sisters frothed at the mouth at the mention of her name that she was their main competition as gossip conduit of Morse Point.

She entered Stan's Diner to find it relatively quiet at midday. Usually she ordered her coffee to go, but today she decided to sit in Marybeth's section and order her latte in-house.

Marybeth was young and pretty with curly brown hair and big blue eyes. She was tall and thin, which was amazing because as Brenna watched her, she noticed that Marybeth nibbled constantly at the food she kept in her polyester apron pockets. It looked like she had a cache of mixed nuts in there, and she reminded Brenna of a squirrel as her eyes darted around the diner before she reached into her pocket to fish out another nut.

"Hi, what can I get for you today?" Marybeth asked with her pad in hand. Brenna noticed she had swallowed before approaching.

Brenna met her gaze over the newspaper she'd been pretending to read and she saw Marybeth's eyes widen in recognition.

"May I have a latte?" she asked.

"Sure," Marybeth said. "Can I offer you some pie as well? We have a freshly baked coconut custard."

"Oh, I'd like that," Brenna said. "Thank you."

Marybeth hesitated as if she wanted to say more but instead she nodded, leaving Brenna's table to go fill the order.

Brenna had spent enough time around the Porter sisters to know that Marybeth was formulating her next run at the table. If she was the gossip everyone claimed, she wouldn't be able to let this opportunity pass, which suited Brenna just fine.

In five minutes, Marybeth was back with the coffee and pie and a winning smile.

"You work over at that paper shop with Tenley Morse, don't you?" she asked.

"That's right," Brenna said. "I'm Brenna Miller."

"Marybeth DeFalco," she said and pointed to her name badge.

"You're married to Officer DeFalco," Brenna said.

"Going on two years," she confirmed. She seemed quite proud of her catch.

"Your husband is very nice," Brenna said. She glanced at the froth on her latte. Today Stan had shaped it into a butterfly.

"He said the same about you," Marybeth said. "He felt just terrible the night that you found the mayor stuffed into that trunk. He said, 'Why did it have to be nice Ms. Miller who found that trunk?'"

"Oh, that's kind of him," Brenna said. "I just wish they'd catch whoever did this."

There, she'd cast her line and now she just had to be patient and reel Marybeth in.

"You don't think it's Mr. Williams?" Marybeth asked.

She glanced over her shoulder to see if Stan was watching them. He was. She began to fuss with the sugar bowl. Brenna didn't want to get her in trouble, so she hurried.

"No," she said quickly. "I'm quite sure it isn't."

Marybeth looked impressed with her certainty.

"I mean there are lots of people who had issues with the mayor, not just Nate," Brenna said. "Why there is . . ."

"Roger Chisholm," Marybeth supplied. "He was hopping mad the day they put that strip mall over the old school. He threatened to chain himself to the school's crumbly old foundation and everything."

"He did?" Brenna encouraged her.

"Oh, yeah." Marybeth nodded. "Until his wife showed up. She scares Roger more than the wrecking ball. She made him put the chains away and go home."

Brenna felt a surge of hope. Just as she had suspected, there were other people with a bone to pick with the mayor.

"And then there is . . ."

"Bart Thompson," Marybeth said. "He found out the mayor was trying to have him put under house arrest on the Fourth of July to prevent his annual streaking problem, and Bart went nuts. He called Ripley a fascist pig and threatened to fill his car with raw bacon."

"Ew," Brenna said. Marybeth shuddered in agreement. "There certainly are a lot of folks who had issues with the mayor."

Marybeth studied her. "Morse Point is a pretty tight community. I think people would rather believe it was a stranger than one of their own. Mr. Williams is still a stranger."

"So am I," Brenna said.

"Yes, but you have Tenley Morse to back you up," she said. "Who does Mr. Williams have?"

"Chief Barker for one," Brenna said. "And me for another."

Marybeth reached into her pocket for a nut while she mulled that over.

"You know who probably has the most information is Ed Johnson," she said. "He's in here all of the time, trying to dig up dirt. I heard he has files on his computer for everyone in town. He even asked around about Cynthia in the beginning, but Phyllis said she was with her, so he let that one go."

"I heard Phyllis was Cynthia's alibi," Brenna said.

"Yeah, those two are like sisters," Marybeth said. "Especially since Phyllis's husband died a few years ago. She's taken Cynthia under her wing."

Brenna was quiet for a moment, considering her words. She decided to be direct. "Do you think Ed knows who killed Mayor Ripley?" she asked.

"No, he'd print that story as soon as he had the proof," Marybeth said. "But I'd be willing to bet he has a good idea about who did it."

"Hmm." Brenna took a bite of her pie. It melted on her tongue in a rich burst of coconut. Yum.

"Let me know if I can get you anything else," Marybeth said. She looked a little disappointed that she hadn't gotten more information out of Brenna. That was okay. Brenna was getting used to letting the gossips down.

She had a bigger problem. She needed to get close to

Ed. She needed to know what he knew. She needed to see his files. And the best way to do that was to get him on his home turf, or better yet, get on his home turf when he wasn't there. The question was how?

"You're kind of phoning it in tonight, aren't you?" Marie Porter asked.

Brenna looked up from the box of photos she was sorting. Her decoupage class at Vintage Papers had started fifteen minutes ago, but only four people had shown up.

The Porter twins, of course; Lillian Page, the librarian at the Morse Point Library; and Sarah Buttercomb, who owned the bakery on the corner. They were always happy when Sarah came to the class because she brought leftover baked goods from work. Tonight she'd brought chocolate-filled, cinnamon-dusted cream puffs, which the Porter twins had been going one for one on all evening.

Conspicuously absent were Cynthia Ripley and Phyllis Portsmyth. Brenna had decided that everyone could just be self-directed on their own projects tonight as her brain was too busy trying to plan how to bust into the *Courier*'s offices.

So far, all she had come up with was trying to bribe the employees in the newspaper office by bringing a box of doughnuts with her and hope they were so distracted by the sugar glaze they didn't notice when she wandered off to snoop. Now, however, she was leaning toward making it a bundt cake. Who could be suspicious of someone bearing a bundt? The dilemma now was what flavor?

"Hello?" Ella waved a hand in front of Brenna's face. "Anyone in there?"

"Huh?" Brenna said. She forced her attention off chocolate with fudge icing versus orange with vanilla icing and focused on the gray-haired woman in front of her, who was giving her a seriously annoyed frown.

"I'm sorry, I'm distracted," Brenna apologized. "I need to get this plaque done for Cynthia Ripley, and it's just not coming together."

It was only a partial lie—given that she was consumed with how to sneak into Ed Johnson's office, she hadn't been able to give the plaque her full attention.

"Well, why don't we make a class project out of it?" Ella offered.

Brenna glanced at Tenley and she shrugged. Brenna took this as a "Why not?" gesture and nodded.

"All right," she said, and she upended the box onto the table. "Let's start by sorting these smallest to largest."

Ella, Marie, Lillian, and Sarah each took a handful of photographs and newspaper clippings and began to organize them.

"How big is the plaque supposed to be?" Marie asked.

"Eleven by seventeen," Brenna said.

"Humph," Ella sniffed.

Brenna ducked her head to keep from laughing. She figured that was Ella's way of saying that Cynthia thought pretty well of herself. She had to agree. In going through the photos, it was impossible not to notice that, other than the picture Ms. Sokolov had given her, Cynthia was in all but one headshot of Mayor Ripley.

"What were your plans for the layout?" Tenley asked.

"I would love to take all these photos and clippings and go totally Warhol with primary colors, et cetera, but I'm thinking Cynthia would be unhappy."

"You think?" Marie asked. Her sarcasm was thicker than the Mod Podge adhesive she'd used on her last project. "Not a lick of artistic ability in that one. Just look at her birdhouse."

Brenna glanced over on the shelf where it sat, looking forlorn. Cynthia had decorated it in fluffy pink kittens wearing big blue bows.

"Well, she did drop it," she said.

"It's still butt ugly," Ella whispered. "Denting the corner just gave it some sorely needed character."

Tenley burst into a coughing fit, no doubt to cover her laughter.

"Yes, well, I promised I'd fix it," Brenna said. "Cynthia wants to hang it in the tree near Mayor Ripley's grave."

"But there aren't any trees near his plot in the cemetery," Lillian, the librarian, said.

She glanced at Brenna through her narrow black-framed glasses. She was in her mid-forties, had five rambunctious boys, six if you counted her husband, and was the most well-read person Brenna had ever met. She wasn't very good at decoupage, and she came to the classes mostly to escape her masculine brood. No one blamed her.

"Really? No trees? I could have sworn that's what she said."

"You must have misheard," Marie said. "Everyone knows all of the mayors are buried on the top of the hill, so they can overlook the town. There aren't any trees planted there; otherwise they couldn't see the town, now could they?"

Brenna frowned. "Maybe Cynthia is having him buried someplace else."

The Porter twins looked at each other and then at her as if she were too stupid to live. Then they looked away,

as if it were just too painful to deal with her city-bred
ignorance. Brenna sighed. As always, fitting in with the
residents of Morse Point was a toe-stomping waltz of one
step forward and twelve steps back.

"Back to the collage," Tenley said, in an obvious attempt to change the subject, for which Brenna was grateful. "If you're not going Warhol, what are you thinking?"

"Honestly, I'm just hoping we can fit all of this onto
the plaque."

"Some of these are too big," Tenley agreed. She was
examining an eight-by-ten of the mayor and Cynthia in
formal attire. "We could take them to the copy store and
have them reduced."

"That would work," Brenna agreed. "Let's separate all
of the pictures that need to be smaller and I'll take them
over as soon as I can."

They made a pile and put them at the end of the worktable. Then Brenna laid out the remaining photos and clippings to see how much room was left.

"It's going to be tight, but I think we can manage it,"
she said.

Ella and Marie looked over her shoulder and clucked
their approval. Lillian and Sarah looked over as well and
nodded in agreement.

Brenna had placed the large headshot of the mayor in
the middle, then using a spiraling technique, she layered
additional photos and clippings to swirl out from the center, leaving blank spots for the photos that needed to be
reduced in size to fit.

"You have a real eye for shape and color," Sarah said.

She leaned close to Brenna to examine the layout, and
a whiff of cinnamon filled the air. Soft-spoken, Sarah was

short and stout and the scent of whatever she had baked
that day often filled the air about her. Brenna always felt
like she was being hugged when she stood next to her.

"You have a gift," Sarah said.

"More like a knack, I think, but thank you," Brenna
said.

"Put that down," Marie snapped.

"No," Ella refused.

Brenna glanced up to see Ella walking away from the
refreshment table with the last of the cream puffs Sarah
had brought from the bakery.

"You have to share," Marie insisted.

"No, I don't," Ella said. "You've already had five. These
are mine."

Brenna exchanged an exasperated look with Tenley.
She had a feeling the twins could get ugly over cream
puffs. She was right.

Marie reached around Ella and tried to snatch a cream
puff off the plate. Ella spun away from her but Marie
caught the edge of the plate with her hand and the cream
puffs were launched catapult style. No one moved as the
tiny pastries spun through the air to land with a splat on
Brenna's layout.

"Now look what you made me do," Ella snapped.

"I made you?" Marie argued. "If you hadn't tried to
hog them all—"

"Ladies," Tenley interrupted. "We have a bigger issue
here. Now take it outside or zip it."

The Porter twins chose to zip it, but this did not prevent them from glowering at one another.

Brenna grabbed a cloth and tried to blot up the cream
filling. The photos were okay but the newspaper clipping
was done for.

"I don't think there's any way to save this clipping," Lillian said. "The ink is beginning to run through and the paper has absorbed chocolate filling."

"I'll have to find another one," Brenna said. "Would the library have the paper back this far?"

"No, I'm afraid not. Ed Johnson is so controlling, he won't let us keep any back issues. We lease our subscription and have to return the papers to him every month."

"You mean you don't have any old issues?" Brenna asked.

"Only a month's worth. For anything older, you have to go to the *Courier* offices," she said.

Brenna stared at Lillian and then she smiled. She couldn't believe it. All of her problems had just been solved by a flying cream puff.

# Chapter 18

Always wipe away any excess glue with a damp sponge but do not disturb the image.

The map was antique looking, printed on firm paper, not as hearty as card stock but not as flimsy as newsprint. The predominant colors were rich browns and reds and showed a cartographer's guess at what the world looked like in the times before Columbus fell upon America. Brenna had been commissioned to cover a small oak table with it.

The main image had gone on smoothly and she was now working on the edging and the legs. Brenna was using squares of matching reds and browns to give the surface a finished look.

The little table had been sitting in her living room for two weeks now, and murder or no murder, Brenna knew her buyer wanted the piece finished soon. She was using a long straight-edged ruler to match the squares at opposite ends of the map. She took the two-by-two-inch squares out of the small bowl of water by her knee and let them drip dry, then she covered the back with a light coating of glue. Carefully, she put the squares on the table, making sure they were aligned, then she used a cloth to gently dab up the excess water and glue. After that, she ran over the squares with her brayer and dabbed at the paper again with the cloth, using the ruler to make sure the squares were still in alignment.

Brenna enjoyed the rhythm of working on a piece. It quieted her mind when she concentrated on the task at hand, and it let her focus more specifically on the millions of questions that flitted through her head. During those dark days after the gallery robbery in Boston, she had worked on numerous pieces both large and small. Looking back, she believed it was the only thing that had kept her sane.

It was easier for her to mull things over when she had something to do with her hands. She considered what Marybeth had told her about Roger Chisholm and Bart Thompson, and she wondered why Ed hadn't gone after them like he did Nate Williams. But, of course, according to Dom, Ed needed to sell papers, and Roger and Bart were of no interest to the world at large. Nate was a celebrity. The mystery that surrounded his departure from the art world made him an enticing murder suspect. Undoubtedly, Ed couldn't resist, especially if it meant saving the *Morse Point Courier*.

Brenna wondered if she should call Dom and see if he could get her into the *Courier* to look around. She hesitated. First, she didn't know Dom that well, and second, bringing in Dom might put Ed on his guard. No, she needed to get into the *Courier* offices when very few people were there and look around unimpeded. She glanced at the chocolate-covered newsprint lying on her counter.

She ran the brayer over a line of squares. She would go
tomorrow night.


Brenna had figured on going into the Courier building alone.
The only problem was Tenley wouldn't let her go without
a lookout. When Brenna protested, her friend got down-
right surly about it and so she reluctantly let Tenley play
lookout again.

It was late evening. Brenna sat in the passenger seat of
Tenley's car, and they waited until most of the *Courier*
staff had departed for dinner. She noticed that the few
who entered the building had swipe badges. She wondered how she was going to get in without one. For good
measure they waited until those who had entered during
their watch left again. Office lights were shut off and there
was an air of abandonment about the place. Now, Brenna
felt confident enough to leave Tenley keeping a lookout in
the car while she hurried across the street to the building.

Brenna stood in the shadows until a photographer banged
out of the main door, talking on his phone while juggling
his camera. Brenna grabbed the door before it shut and
slipped inside.

There was a peculiar smell to the offices of the *Morse
Point Courier*. Brenna tried to place it, but all she came up
with was a mixture of sweat, rancid coffee, and printer's
ink.

A light at the end of a short hall led her to the main
newsroom. Most of the cubicles sat empty. She wandered
through the sea of abandoned desks until she reached the
one office in the room that had a door. It belonged to John
Sheady, the night editor.

John was a little over six feet tall and everything about

him was gray. His hair, his dingy dress shirt, his charcoal slacks, even his skin under the pulsing fluorescent lights appeared to be a pearly shade of gray. John had been the night editor for fifteen years, and Brenna wondered if this was what a life without daylight did to a person.

He glanced up from his computer. He appeared grumpy and annoyed at the interruption, but when she explained about the plaque, he nodded in understanding.

"I went to grade school with Jim," he said. "He wasn't my favorite person, but he sure deserved better than this. I can't imagine what Chief Barker was thinking letting that crazy artist out of jail when he's obviously a sociopath."

"He is not," Brenna snapped.

John looked at her and Brenna pressed her lips together. She had to play this very carefully; otherwise she'd be tossed out on her posterior before she had a chance to look for any evidence.

"What I mean is, 'innocent until proven guilty.' Right?" she asked.

"So, what is it that you need exactly?" John asked. He looked less helpful than he had a minute ago and Brenna figured she'd better smooth it over.

"A copy of the article about Ripley being sworn in as mayor," she said. "One of my students splatted a cream puff all over the original."

John Sheady took the chocolate-crusted clipping out of her hand and grimaced. "You're lucky the date is still legible."

"I know," she said.

"We have old issues on hard copy and on microfilm. I'll get you the hard copy. It'll make a better print for what you're doing."

"Thank you," she said.

"Look, I have to proof the layouts for tonight's print run," he said. "I can show you the archive room and the copiers and then you're on your own."

Brenna wanted to do a happy dance, but she settled for smiling and nodding instead.

John led her back through the maze of cubicles to a room in the back of the building. The temperature dropped to a frigid fifty-eight degrees, and Brenna knew it was to preserve the papers that had yet to be put on film.

John checked the date on the clipping and then led her to the compact shelving. He hit a button to make the shelves move over. A grinding noise began, and one by one the shelves slid over toward the right wall.

Once they stopped, John stepped in between them and pulled out an archival box of newspapers.

"The one you're looking for is in here," he said. He glanced at his watch. "I have to start proofing. The copier is down the hall to your right, in front of Ed's office. When you're done, leave the papers in the box here. I'll put them away."

Brenna suspected that was his way of being sure that she didn't steal anything. She was just tickled that he had handed her the golden ticket, an unsupervised visit to Ed's office.

She dug into the papers, looking for the one she needed. He was gone a mere two minutes when she found the article. She left the freezing room behind and headed down the hallway.

The copier in front of Ed's office was off. She switched it on and then hurried back down the hall to look over the newsroom. John's office was located on the other side, past the sea of cubicles. There was no way he could see her from here and no one else appeared to be in the building.

She hurried back to the copier. She lifted the lid, but it was still warming up. She leaned her back against Ed's office door and turned the knob with her hand. It opened with a muffled click.

Brenna pushed the door slowly backward, hoping its hinges weren't squeaky. The door slid silently across the blue industrial carpet, and she breathed a sigh of relief. She turned and slowly closed the door behind her.

She pulled her cell phone out of her pocket and called Tenley, who picked up on the first ring.

"What's your twenty?" she asked. Obviously, she'd been watching too many cop shows.

"I'm in," Brenna said.

"Roger that," Tenley said, and then she giggled. Brenna rolled her eyes, although there was no one there to see her, and hung up.

They had worked it out that if Tenley saw anyone enter the building, she would call Brenna's cell phone, which was set to vibrate, to warn her. If Ed entered the building, she would call her once, hang up, and call her again to let her know he was on his way.

Brenna kept the office light off and worked by the glow of Ed's screen saver, which was the header of the *Morse Point Courier* being typed across the screen in a continuous loop.

A cursory glance was all she needed to see that Ed was a pig. A blackened banana and empty carryout containers littered the top of his desk, which was piled eye high with reams of paper, folders, and Post-it notes. Good grief, how was she supposed to find anything in here if she didn't even know what she was looking for?

She glanced out the window of the office. There was no movement. She felt jittery and jumpy, expecting to be caught at any moment. The harder she tried to figure out where to start, the more paralyzed she felt.

"Knock it off, Brenna," she whispered to herself. "Come on, focus."

She closed her eyes and breathed in through her nose and out through her mouth. Feeling a smidge calmer, she figured the best starting place was his desk. She began to flip through the stacks, being careful not to move anything in case Ed was one of those people who knew exactly where everything in his personal mess was.

She tried to read his notes but his handwriting looked more like hieroglyphics than anything else. She shuffled through several piles of minutes from the latest town council meetings, the schedule for the peewee football league, and the take-out menus from eight nearby restaurants.

She glanced back through the window again—still no sign of anyone. She shifted to the left side of his desk and began to riffle through those papers, while holding a congealed cup of coffee from Stan's Diner in her left hand to keep from spilling it. Ew.

Still, there was nothing. She tapped the space bar on his keyboard to see if she could access the files Marybeth had mentioned. She scanned the icons, but saw nothing that looked like what she wanted. She double-clicked an e-mail icon. His e-mail log-in window filled the screen.

His first initial and last name were already in the log-in space, but the password line was empty. She tried the obvious and put in his first initial and last name in the password line. She was rejected. Then she tried the name of the paper. Nothing.

What would Ed use as a password? She glanced at his desk. There were no photos of people or pets. On the wall were framed photos of him at several area press club banquets, but there were no awards on the shelf.

The one thing Ed craved more than anything was recognition. It was a long shot, but she tried it anyway. In the password line she typed "Pulitzer," and Ed's e-mail opened up like an oyster spitting out a pearl.

Brenna resisted the urge to pump her fist, barely. She scanned through his in-box. There were lots of local messages about events happening in Morse Point; several more were from New York and had Nate Williams as the subject line. It killed her to skip these, but she knew they were just gossip. She thought about deleting them, but knew that would be crossing an ethical line she was not yet ready to jump over.

She worked from older to newer, starting with the day Ripley was murdered. There had to be something in here that would give a clue as to who Ed thought was the murderer or even if it was Ed himself. She still hadn't given up the idea that he might have had something to do with the mayor's demise. Ed did not strike her as the sharpest pencil in the box—he had to have left some clue, made some misstep, something.

Toward the top of his in-box, she saw a message with no subject line. She opened it.

It read: *I know who murdered Mayor Ripley. Meet me at the Willow House at 9:00 pm. Come alone.*

It was dated today.

Just then, her phone vibrated in her pocket and she jumped. She knocked the congealed coffee cup with her hand and sludge oozed out across the desk.

"Damn it," she hissed. Her phone stopped vibrating. She had to get out of there.

She hit print and bounced on her feet as the printer

slowly ground out the message. She exited out of Ed's e-mail, snatched the page from the printer, and hurried out to the copier. It was ready now. She ran a quick copy of the article she needed. As the copier hummed and its green glow lit up the hallway, she felt her phone vibrate again.

Oh no, that was two calls. That meant Ed was on his way.

She grabbed her copy and the original and dashed down the hall to the archive room. She stuffed the newspaper in the box and hurried back through the newsroom toward John Sheady's office. She found him sipping a steaming cup of coffee.

"Thanks so much, John," she said. She forced a smile even though she felt as if her heart was going to pound right through her rib cage.

"Sure," he said. "Did it copy all right?"

She glanced at the copy in her hand without really seeing it. The phone in her pocket was still vibrating. She was out of time!

"Yeah, it looks great," she said, backing toward the door. "Thanks and, uh, bye."

She turned and broke into a run.

# Chapter 19

To sharpen edges or add colors, use a pen and ink or a thin marker.

Brenna broke through the main doors to find Tenley in her Honda Pilot with the engine running. Brenna hopped into the passenger's seat and Tenley sped from the curb.

"I'm sorry," Tenley said.

"For what?"

"It was a false alarm," Tenley said. "I saw Ed walking down the street towards the building, so I called twice but he didn't go in. He climbed into his car and took off."

"That's okay," Brenna said. "Because we're going to follow him."

"What? How? I didn't see where he went," Tenley said.

"What and where is the Willow House?" Brenna asked, while she fumbled with her seatbelt.

"It's a student hangout on the edge of town, near the university," Tenley said. "Why?"

Brenna glanced at her watch. It was eight thirty. They only had thirty minutes.

"How fast can you get us there?"

"If I hit the lights right, twenty-five minutes," she said. She stomped on the accelerator and Brenna reflexively grabbed her armrest.

Tenley glanced at her. "What's going on?"

"I found this in Ed's office," she said and read her the e-mail.

"Should we call Chief Barker?" Tenley asked.

There was a beat of silence.

"I am going to hope that Ed had the good sense to do just that," Brenna said. A thought struck her. "Unless Ed is the guilty party."

"You think someone is calling Ed out?"

"Maybe," Brenna said. "We need to see who is meeting Ed then we'll call Chief Barker."

They hit three lights, which set them back a few minutes. After twice circling the 1920s residential house that had been converted into a coffee shop, it became apparent there was no parking. Tenley pulled over to let Brenna out.

The coffeehouse was full to bursting with students, and it was standing room only as a live band was performing outside on the terrace. The bass beat of the drum was so loud that it made glasses skitter across table tops. The lead singer was a shrieker, performing what they called screamo. It certainly made Brenna want to scream with frustration. How were they supposed to track Ed Johnson in this crush of people?

She jostled her way through the crowd, getting bumped as she made her way toward the door. If Ed was meeting someone to talk, he'd want to do it where it was quieter.

A tie-dyed T-shirt flitted by her and she glanced up to see an older man with a long, gray ponytail dancing by.

His arms were raised, his butt was pushed out, and he alternated stomping his feet in time with the beat. He was the worst dancer she'd ever seen. Just then, he glanced up and she recognized Bart Thompson. He gave her a big smile and a wave and danced over to her side.

"Inhale-Exhale-Repeat! Aren't they great?" he yelled in her ear as he pointed a thumb at the band. Brenna nodded.

He bounced at her side, seemingly off in his own world. She supposed it was a long shot, but she asked anyway, "Bart, have you seen Ed Johnson?"

Bart tilted his head to the side and looked puzzled. "I don't really think this is his scene," he said. Then his face lit up. "Hey, do you think he'd take my picture for the paper?"

Just then Twyla appeared out of the crush. She was dressed in a vibrant shade of purple and draped in crystals. Her lined face split into a grin when she saw Brenna, and she wrapped her into a crusher hug.

"I didn't know you were going to be here," Twyla said. "We could have driven together."

Bart was dancing on his own just a few feet away from them.

Curiosity overwhelmed her and Brenna asked, "Are you two dating?"

Twyla's eyes twinkled and she said, "Sometimes."

Brenna wondered why she hadn't seen it before. They were a perfect pair.

"Do you want to dance with us, dear?" Twyla asked.

"Thanks, but I'm meeting someone," Brenna lied. Twyla nodded in understanding and gave her a wink. She wrapped her hand around Bart's arm and they gave Brenna a wave as they were absorbed into the crush.

Brenna scanned the area for familiar faces, but saw
no one other than Bart and Twyla. She pushed her way
through the crowd and up the stairs. Once inside, the
crowd lessened somewhat, and she hurried into the main
room. Every table was full, but there was still no sign of
Ed.

She searched three more rooms, until she reached the
back door. Outside, she noticed the back patio of the house
was full of tables as well. She scanned the tables, but
there was still no sign of him.

A block wall encircled the small grassy yard. A cob-
bled walkway led through the grass to a short wrought-
iron gate at the back of the yard. The gate hung open as
if someone had just walked through it. Maybe the noise
had driven Ed and his contact to a quieter spot beyond
the grounds. She jogged across the lawn and through the
gate.

She pushed it open and carefully stepped through. It
led to an alley, which was too dark to cast shadows and
pungent with the acrid smell of rotten milk.

It was quieter out here, the band muffled by the block
wall behind her. She glanced in both directions, but without a street light, it was impossible to see farther than an
arm's length away.

She heard a noise to her right, and she started. It
sounded like a hiss, and she thought it was probably a tom
cat. Still, the hair on the back of her neck stood up in
alarm.

She took a breath and walked toward the sound. Her
foot connected with something solid and yet soft. She
jumped back with a yelp. Her breath was coming short
and fast, but she forced herself to kneel and reach out with
her hand. If it was an injured animal, she knew she'd get

clawed. But if it was something else . . . she refused to think about it.

She patted the jagged pavement, her fingers trembling, when she touched fabric. She wanted to pull her hand back, but she didn't. Instead she stretched out her fingers. There was no mistaking the feel of a human leg beneath her hand. Brenna knew she had found Ed Johnson.

She scrambled up toward his head. She could hear herself breathing loudly through her nose as she tried to keep herself upright with bracing gusts of oxygen.

She ran her hands over his face. There was a warm sticky liquid on his temple that she suspected was blood, and she felt faint breaths being emitted from between his lips. He was breathing. She put her hand on his chest and measured the rise and fall. It was faint but steady.

"Brenna!" She heard Tenley call her name and she turned toward the gate.

"Over here!" she yelled. "I found him. He's badly hurt but still breathing."

The gate swung wide and Tenley, Bart, and Twyla rushed to her side. Tenley pressed the miniflashlight on her keychain. She swept the light up Ed's body until it shone on his face. Pale with blood oozing out of a nasty gash over his eye, Ed looked pretty bad.

"Holy crap!" Bart exclaimed. "Is he dead?"

"Oh, no, not again," Twyla whimpered.

"He's not dead. Call an ambulance," Brenna said and Tenley dug her phone out of her purse.

"I'll go tell the manager," Twyla said, and she bolted in a flurry of purple back inside.

Tenley told the dispatcher where they were and stayed on the line. She leaned close to Brenna and asked, "Are you all right?"

"Yeah, I think so. Better than Ed, at any rate," she said. "Thank God he's alive. I don't think I could handle two bodies in as many weeks."

Ed groaned and Brenna leaned close. "Ed, can you hear me?"

"The plate doesn't match," he mumbled. "No match."

"What plate?" she asked. "Ed, who hit you? Ed?"

His eyes opened just a crack and then they rolled back into his head as a shudder rippled through his body. Brenna checked his pulse; it was thready but still there.

"The ambulance is on its way," Tenley said.

The manager of the Willow House bustled out into the alley with Twyla. He brought several clean towels and Brenna used one to wipe her hands. She would have liked to clean up Ed's head wound, but she was afraid to move him, so she held a towel to it to staunch the blood flow until the paramedics arrived.

In just minutes the ambulance arrived with its siren blaring, effectively shutting down the screaming band. The medics took over monitoring Ed's vitals and loaded him onto a stretcher. Sadly, Brenna and the others could offer no information as to what had happened to Ed and the paramedics whisked him away to the hospital for further tests.

"Well, if you ladies will excuse me," Bart said, "I need to be going. Sirens make me twitchy."

"Me, too," Twyla agreed.

Brenna and Tenley watched as they disappeared back into the coffeehouse.

As the crowd dispersed, Brenna and Tenley headed to Tenley's car, which was parked around the corner from the coffee shop.

They were halfway there when a police car pulled up

beside them and Chief Barker jumped out, looking half-crazy. Brenna wasn't positive, but his mustache looked thinner, as if he'd been pulling it out in frustrated tufts.

"Not for nothing, but can either of you tell me just what the Sam Hell you were doing in the alley?" he barked.

Uh-oh. Did he know they'd been looking for Ed?

Brenna exchanged a look with Tenley. Tenley gave her a small nod and Brenna fished the e-mail out of her pocket and handed it to Chief Barker.

His hand went reflexively to his mustache, which he tugged while he read. When he glanced up, he said, "I believe it is time for us to sit and have a talk."

"Do you want to sit out here?" Brenna asked, gesturing to the now empty outside tables.

"No," he said. "I was thinking more along the lines of the police station."

# Chapter 20

Sealants will preserve the decoupage piece and can be applied in as few as two coats or as many as thirty.

Brenna caught a glimpse of Tenley's face, which went paler than a sheet of starwhite paper as Officer DeFalco joined them. Tenley went with him, while Chief Barker motioned for Brenna to come with him.

His squad car was parked at the corner, and he held the back door open for her. Brenna had never been in a police car in her life. She knew she had done nothing wrong—well, she hadn't murdered anyone at any rate—but still she felt guilt cramp her conscience.

She wondered what kind of trouble she would be in for snooping in Ed's office at the paper. Wouldn't it actually be a help to the police? First, it proved that Ed wasn't the murderer, which was a good thing, and second, it could help the police track down Ed's attacker.

Brenna was sure it had to be the murderer. Whoever had sent the e-mail had to be the same person who murdered Mayor Ripley. But why did they go after Ed? He'd been using his paper to smear Nate and make him look like the killer, unless Nate was . . . no, absolutely not. She refused to believe it.

"Anything you care to share?" Chief Barker asked.

Brenna glanced up and realized he'd been watching her in the rearview mirror.

"Nope," she said. "Just humming a song in my head."

"Uh-huh." He shook his head, and she knew he didn't believe her. This promised to be a long night.


Three hours passed with Chief Barker asking the same questions again and again until finally Brenna was free to go. She'd said she did not recall so many times, she was sure she must be running for public office. That Chief Barker was unhappy with her, she had no doubt. She liked the chief and felt badly about that, but she gave him only the pertinent facts. The rest he would have to figure out on his own.

It wasn't that she meant to be unhelpful. She just didn't want to pull Tenley into a bad situation because of her decisions, and until she talked to her, she didn't feel right giving anything more than the facts.

Tenley was waiting for her out in the hallway when she was finally dismissed. The two friends hugged.

"Your parents are going to be so unhappy when they hear about this," Brenna said.

Tenley said something that was muffled against her shoulder, and Brenna was worried it might be a sob. She released her friend and pulled back to study her face. To her surprise, Tenley was grinning.

"I wish I could see their faces," she chortled. "This is going to make my dating Matt in high school seem like small potatoes."

Then she laughed again and Brenna couldn't help but chuckle in return. Aware that they were getting odd looks from the officer on desk duty, they ducked their heads and exited the police station, not letting loose their laughter until they were outside the building and around the corner. There they laughed until tears formed in their eyes and their bellies hurt.

That it was a nervous reaction from the night's events, Brenna had no doubt. Still, every time she glanced at Tenley, she dissolved into a fit of the giggles.

Finally, when they were too weak to laugh anymore, they slumped against the exterior brick wall and let the cool night air wash over them. There was a faint scent of exhaust on the breeze, and Brenna realized they were standing near the police parking lot. She could only imagine what Chief Barker would make of this if he saw the two of them.

"I think we've hit delirious," she said. "Let's walk back to Vintage Papers and get my car. I'll drive you home. We can pick up your car tomorrow."

Twenty minutes later, she left Tenley at her apartment, the second story of an old house on the edge of the town square, and was heading back to her cabin. She wondered if Twyla had made it home okay, or if the police had found her and Bart at the Willow House and brought them in for questioning as well.

When Brenna pulled into the communal lot, Bart's yellow pickup truck was parked in her spot. Twyla's old station wagon was there as well, so she figured they'd avoided being questioned. She remembered Bart's face when they found Ed. She didn't think he was a good enough actor to pull off his look of shock. She didn't think Bart had planned to meet Ed, nor did she think he had murdered the mayor.

She thought back to the coffeehouse. She hadn't seen

Roger Chisholm there, although he could easily have been amid the crowd. It had certainly been mobbed enough that he could have gone undetected. If Bart hadn't been wearing such a loud shirt, she might never have seen him.

She knew Chief Barker would investigate who had attacked Ed, but she was afraid the panic caused by another attack would force the chief to reconsider Nate. He hadn't been at the coffeehouse; she would have known. Given the suspicions that surrounded him already, everyone would have known if Nate had been there.

She was glad she had told the chief about the e-mail, but like a loose thread, it niggled at her. Who had wanted to meet Ed? Was it the killer, drawing him out because he was getting too close? What did Ed know that had made him a target? Someone wanted to silence him, but why? If she could just figure out who had sent Ed that e-mail, she knew she would discover the mayor's killer.

She keyed into her cabin and glanced at the clock on her kitchen wall. It was after one in the morning. The only people up now were insomniacs or the night editors of newspapers.

She grabbed yesterday's copy of the *Morse Point Courier* and strode over to the cordless phone on the counter. On the inside of page one, she scanned the list of editors until she found John Sheady's name. She dialed the phone number listed by his name.

"Sheady," he answered abruptly on one ring.

"Hi, John, it's Brenna Miller," she said.

"Oh." He processed that for a second. "I thought you might be the doc at the hospital."

"Is there any word on Ed yet?" she asked.

"He's stable," he said. "I heard from Officer DeFalco that you were the one who found him."

"Yeah," she said. Her voice came out shakier than she'd expected.

"How did you know?" he asked.

"I found an e-mail in his office," she said. Brenna figured lying wasn't an option. Not if she wanted any cooperation.

"You might have mentioned that when you were here," he said. His voice was chastising and Brenna cringed.

"I might have," she said. "But I sort of figured he'd be getting coffee, not a concussion."

"Fair enough," Sheady said. "So why are you calling me now?"

"I'm sure the police have already asked you this," Brenna said, "but do you have any idea who Ed might have been meeting?"

"Why do you want to know?" he asked.

"Because I was in the coffeehouse," she said. "I saw a lot of people. If there is someone that has been making contact with Ed, maybe I saw them, maybe I can help catch whoever did this to him."

"Hunh," John grunted. Brenna could tell he was thinking over what she said. "I can only tell you what I already told the police. As far as I know, Ed believed that Nate Williams killed the mayor and he was doing everything in his power to prove it."

Brenna felt her heart thunk like a stone in her chest. This did not look good for Nate.

"So, there was no one else calling him or trying to see him?" she asked.

"Only Eleanor Sokolov," John said. "She came by three times to see him yesterday, but he gave her the bum's rush."

"The mayor's secretary came by?" Brenna asked. "Why?"

"I don't know," he said. "I wasn't here. I only heard about it later."

"Thanks, John," Brenna said. "You've been a big help."

"Sure," he said and hung up with a click.

Brenna stared at the phone in her hand. What could Eleanor possibly want with Ed, unless she knew something? Brenna was going to find out what, first thing tomorrow morning, even if she had to threaten her with another fire extinguisher to do it.

She got ready for bed, thinking she'd never sleep. Instead it was a short race between her and the lamp on her nightstand to see who was out first. Brenna won.

The town hall officially opened at eight. Brenna was there at seven thirty. She was hoping she could sweet-talk Abner, the guard, into letting her in.

She pressed her nose against the window in the back door, hoping to catch the guard if he went by. There was no sign of him. Only a handful of cars were parked in the lot at the back of the building. She wondered if one of them belonged to Ms. Sokolov.

As she was pondering this, the back door swung open. She turned back with her most charming smile on her face, hoping to soften Abner. Instead, her smile faltered as she took in Ms. Sokolov.

"Do you have my picture?" she snapped. She was wearing another polyester ruffle blouse in a bold shade of fuchsia with a pleated black skirt. Her lipstick matched the blouse, and the overall picture was overwhelming.

Caught off guard, Brenna stammered, "Uh, n—no."

"Then why are you here?" Ms. Sokolov asked. "The town hall doesn't open for another half hour."

Brenna decided finesse would be wasted on a person of such bluntness, so she went right to the point. "Why were you calling Ed Johnson repeatedly?"

Ms. Sokolov reared back as if she'd taken a swing at her. Obviously, this was not what she had expected.

"Why do you ask?"

"Someone tried to kill him last night."

"Oh, my," Ms. Sokolov said, fiddling with one of the ruffles on her cuff. She looked rattled, but she pulled herself up straight and glared at Brenna. "I don't see how my calling Ed Johnson is any of your business."

"I'm the one who found him bleeding in an alley," Brenna said. "That makes it my business." Okay, not really. But she was hoping it would stall an argument.

"You surely don't think I had anything to do with it," Ms. Sokolov said, looking outraged.

Brenna gave her a hard stare.

Ms. Sokolov drew herself up to her full height, which put her in the vicinity of Brenna's nose.

"How dare you," she said. "I am a respectable citizen. I would never harm a soul. You, however—I know all about you."

Brenna stepped back as if she'd touched a hot stove. Her stomach cramped and a sick feeling of dread coated her skin like a rash.

"Oh, yes, you might well look shame-faced," Ms. Sokolov continued. "I know all about that gallery robbery in which you were the prime suspect. If the police should question anyone, it's you. Why, we never had a problem with crime in Morse Point until you showed up."

"My past isn't relevant," Brenna gritted out, but even to her own ears, her voice sounded weak. "Why were you trying to get in touch with Ed?"

"Because I wrote the mayor's eulogy," Ms. Sokolov said. "And I wanted Ed to proofread it for me. Satisfied?"

To Brenna's shock, Ms. Sokolov burst into tears and slammed the door in her face. She stood there gaping for a second before she walked back to her car on rubbery knees.

She had no doubt that if Ms. Sokolov knew about Boston, then everyone did. That didn't sit well with her, but there wasn't much she could do about it right now.

Brenna gathered the folder of pictures from her Jeep and ambled over to the copy store, trying not to think about what a colossal failure her interview with Ms. Sokolov had been.

She didn't want to admit that Eleanor's cruel words had gotten to her, but to call her surly would have been a dramatic understatement. The only person suffering an uglier mood swing than Brenna was the disgruntled youth behind the copy store counter, who sported a nose ring and an inability to make eye contact.

"I need these reproduced to a quarter of their original size with a matte finish. Is that possible?"

"Anything is possible," he said with a heavy sigh.

Brenna glanced at his nametag. "Well, Chad, how long do you suppose that would take?"

"If you want to pay extra, they can be done in an hour," he said.

"Fine," she agreed.

She used her cell phone to check her messages. Cynthia had left one yesterday evening telling her that Jim's body had been released by the medical examiner and that the funeral would be held the day after next. If she was going to have the plaque ready for the viewing, she had to get it done today.

While she waited for Chad to write up the order, she laid the pictures out on the counter. There were five of them. She knew exactly where she was going to put each one in the collage, balancing the colors and backgrounds. As she signed the order form, she glanced over the picture of Jim and Cynthia in formal wear. It was the largest of the five and would need to be cropped to fit in the collage, even if it was reduced. She studied the picture, trying to determine where she should crop it.

An object in the bottom-left corner caught her eye. She felt her heart rate accelerate and her breathing became quick.

"Excuse me," she called over the counter to Chad, who was fiddling with some prints coming out of the behemoth machine in front of him. "Can you enlarge this for me?"

"I thought you wanted everything reduced," he replied, looking put-upon.

"I did. I do, but I need an enlargement, too," she said.

"It'll cost more," he said, as if bracing himself for an argument.

"That's fine, but can you do it right now?" she asked.

"Lady, that's a rush job," he said as if she were asking him to hand-paint a portrait on the spot.

Brenna bit down her impatience, forced a smile, and said, "That's okay, I'll pay extra."

He shuffled over to the counter and she handed him the picture.

"I just need the bottom-left corner blown up," she said.

"But that's their feet, not their heads," he said.

"I'm aware," she said. "Just do it, please, and hurry."

He gave her a look that said more clearly than words that he thought she was cracked, but Brenna didn't care. If she was right, and she was pretty sure she was, then she had just figured out who killed Jim Ripley.

Within fifteen minutes, Chad handed her the print she needed. She took it out into the sunlight to study it. There was no question.

Sitting unobtrusively in the photo behind Jim was the same trunk he'd been stuffed into when Brenna had pulled him out of the lake. She recognized the shiny brass hardware and burgundy leather trim. Smiling next to him in the photo was his adoring wife and, she suspected, killer, Cynthia Ripley.

# Chapter 21

An oil-based sealant may yellow with age, giving the piece an antique look.

Brenna stood clutching the photo. Her heart was banging around in her chest like a rock in a tire. Now what? Did she take the photo to Chief Barker and tell him what she knew? But how could she prove it? He was still pretty ticked about last night. Did she really want to face his wrath this early in the morning? Uh, that was a no.

Besides, with Ed in the hospital, he might brush off what she'd discovered, thinking it unimportant. That would be bad. Then again, she could be wrong and that would be worse.

She studied the photo. Judging by the bookcases, the trunk, and the dark paneling in the photo, it looked to have been taken in a home library. She figured it must be the Ripleys' house. Now if she could get into the house and make sure the trunk wasn't there, she'd know for sure.

Without hesitation, she climbed into her Jeep and

headed for their Laurel Hill address on the wealthy side of town.

As she drove, she tried to think of a legitimate excuse to be popping in on Cynthia Ripley. The plaque, of course, was the only thing that made sense. She would ask Cynthia if it was all right if she reduced a few of the photos, an artistic issue—that seemed plausible.

She wound her way up the hill, past the Morse and Portsmyth estates. The battle for the title of most prominent family waged steadily up here on the hill, as was evidenced by their landscaping.

Tenley's mother had her Canada yew shrubs cut into the shape of sitting lions, like those outside the New York Public Library, and they loomed over the winding entrance to the mansion beyond. The Portsmyths' gardener had attempted to match this by shaping enormous boxwood shrubs into the form of two elephants standing on their hind legs with trunks intertwined, making an arch over the drive.

It would have been impressive, except for the fact that it appeared that one of the elephants was missing a chunk out of its derriere. Brenna glanced back at the lions. Yep, one of the lions had a suspicious tangle of boxwood hanging out of its mouth. Apparently, the Morse and Portsmyth rivalry extended to their gardeners.

A beat-up red pickup truck zipped out of the Portsmyth driveway, forcing Brenna to slam on her brakes or risk ramming him. At the wheel of the truck was Patrick O'Shea, Phyllis's gardener. The bed of his pickup was loaded with equipment, and Brenna watched as he spun gravel and parked in front of the Morses' drive.

He climbed out of the truck wielding a pair of ominous-looking shears. She watched, in stunned silence, as he stood

on the hood of his truck and lopped off the head of the
lion with the elephant's butt in its mouth.

Then he waved his fist at the Morse estate and yelled,
"That's for costing me my job, you rat bastard!"

He climbed back in his truck and sped off, not even
sparing Brenna a glance. She scanned the area and stepped
on the gas, fearing someone might see her and think she
was the lion head lopper-offer.

The Ripley mansion was on the backside of the hill, an
address of lesser prominence befitting a mansion of lesser
square footage. Brenna turned into the drive, noting that
there were no shrub animals, maimed or otherwise, to
greet her.

Cynthia's Escalade was parked in the circular drive in
front of the house. Good. She was home. Brenna noticed
that her hands were slick with sweat. Confrontations were
not her specialty.

Uncertainty flooded her as she wondered what exactly
she hoped to get out of this. A teary confession? A hot de-
nial? Or just confirmation of her own suspicions? Oh yeah,
that was it. She wanted to prove that Cynthia was indeed the
murderer. She felt weak in the knees and thought maybe she
should have had more fiber in her breakfast this morning.

An older woman, wearing a serviceable gray dress
with a white Peter Pan collar and a crisp white apron, answered the door when Brenna pressed the bell. Her face
was impassive, expressing neither annoyance nor welcome
at the sight of her.

"Good morning, ma'am, may I help you?" she asked.
Her voice was not exactly robotic but it was as if any hint
of emotion had been bleached from it like a stain from her
apron.

Brenna wondered if this was something taught in the

domestic arts or if years spent waiting upon other people had slowly eroded any emotion from her until there was nothing left.

"Hi, I'm Brenna Miller. I'm working on a memorial plaque for Mrs. Ripley and I . . ." Brenna trailed off under the woman's unblinking stare. She was babbling and yet the woman didn't cut her off or encourage her. It was very unnerving.

"Who is it, Grace?" a voice Brenna recognized as Cynthia's called from inside the house.

"A Ms. Brenna Miller," Grace answered, turning slightly so that her voice would carry.

"Please show her in," Cynthia called.

"If you'll follow me, ma'am." Grace moved aside to let Brenna in.

She stepped into an austere marble foyer, done in rich earth tones. A fragile wooden table stood in the center of the rounded entrance with an ornate ceramic bowl of fruit placed on it. Brenna couldn't tell if the fruit was real or not as she passed, which she found bothersome.

She realized that this was likely her best opportunity to snoop for the paneled room with the trunk. As she followed Grace down the hall, she craned her neck to peer into the rooms they passed.

The sitting room, first door on the left, was yellow trimmed with white and decorated with sunflowers on the drapes and upholstery. A small office followed that on her right, done in a nautical theme of navy blue and red. A staircase was tucked into the wall beyond, and Brenna knew she had no hope of going up there unless she was invited.

They passed the entrance to the kitchen, all brushed steel and mottled granite, and then Grace paused at a door that stood slightly ajar on the right. She gave it a light rap and pushed it open.

Brenna entered a bright room, done in masculine green stripes with a matching lush green carpet. Tall windows, along one wall, boasted a magnificent view of the back lawns, and two brown leather wing chairs were placed in front of a fireplace, which was framed by floor-to-ceiling bookshelves. There was not a strip of paneling to be seen. Nuts.

Cynthia rose from the desk that sat in front of the window and came around it with her hand extended. She was still in her bathrobe and her hair looked knotted as if she hadn't combed it in days. Brenna felt a twinge of unease. What if she was wrong and she was intruding upon Cynthia's grief with her suspicions? But then maybe it was guilt gnawing at her that made Cynthia look so disheveled. Brenna straightened her back.

"Hello, Brenna." Cynthia clasped her hand in between her cold ones. The contact made Brenna shiver. "Is it done then?"

"Is what done?"

"The plaque?" Cynthia released her hands.

"What? Oh, no, not quite," Brenna said.

Cynthia frowned at her, looking less welcoming by the second. "There isn't a problem, is there?"

"No, no problem," she said. There was an awkward pause and she rushed on, "I did want your permission to reduce a couple of the photos."

"Reduce?" Cynthia asked.

They remained standing. It appeared Cynthia would not be asking her to stay and visit. Hmm.

"Just to make them fit more easily into the plaque," Brenna said.

"You're the artist, do as you will. Just make sure it's done in time," Cynthia said. Her voice was short and tight. "I don't mean to be rude, but I have so much to do to plan Jim's funeral. I'm sure you understand."

Brenna pretended not to. "I like what you've done with this room. I always think of home offices as being dark-paneled rooms without windows, maybe done in burgundy."

"Hmm," Cynthia muttered, moving toward the door.

"Ever consider anything like that for this room?" Brenna asked.

"No, I loathe paneling," Cynthia said. "It's much too stuffy. I wouldn't have it in my house."

"Really?" Brenna asked. "Not in any room?"

Cynthia gave her a piercing look. "Why are you so interested in my decorating?"

"Oh, just making small talk," Brenna said. It sounded lame even to her.

"Don't trouble yourself," Cynthia said. It wasn't a suggestion. "Was there anything else?"

"No, no, I just wanted your approval."

"You have it," Cynthia said. "Grace, please show Ms. Miller out and please try to be more quiet with your cleaning. I have had a raging stress headache ever since I talked to Chief Barker this morning."

Grace appeared abruptly as if she'd been waiting outside the door, but Brenna ignored her.

"What did the chief have to say?" Brenna asked.

"That Nate Williams is still walking around free," Cynthia said. "I know he murdered my husband, and I'm sure he attacked Ed Johnson as well. I am going to see that man behind bars if it's the last thing I do."

"But . . . ." Brenna began to protest, but Cynthia held up

her hand for silence. "If you'll excuse me, I'm feeling quite ill."

Left with no other options, Brenna was escorted to the front door by the housekeeper.

Brenna wondered how loyal Grace was to Cynthia. It seemed Cynthia could be quite demanding. She knew it was a long shot but she had to try.

"Grace, may I ask you something?" They had reached the front door and Grace looked ready to toss Brenna to the curb.

"Yes, ma'am," she said.

"Do you recognize the trunk in this picture?" she asked.

Grace gave her an uncertain look, but took the photo in her hand to study it.

"No, I'm afraid I don't," she said and handed the photo back.

"So, the Ripleys have never owned one like it?"

"No, ma'am."

"One more question?" she asked.

Grace nodded.

"How did the Ripleys get along? I mean, were they happy?"

Grace looked over her shoulder as if expecting Cynthia to appear. "They seemed happy," she said. "Until the night he was murdered."

"Why do you say that?" Brenna asked.

Grace looked uncertain, as if afraid she'd said too much. "I really need to get back, ma'am."

"Please, Grace," Brenna said. "It's important."

Grace stared at her for moment, and Brenna met her gaze, trying to will the housekeeper to tell her anything she knew that might help.

"I don't suppose it's out of line to tell you what I've already told the police," Grace said. "The Ripleys had a terrible fight the night he died. They even dismissed me for the night and told me to take a paid holiday. That never happens."

"Was anyone else here?" Brenna asked.

"No one," Grace said. "Honestly, when I first heard the mayor had been murdered, I thought it was Mrs. Ripley, but she has a solid alibi."

"Yes, she was with Phyllis Portsmyth," Brenna said. "Grace, do you think Mrs. Ripley killed her husband?"

"I don't honestly kn—"

"Grace!" Cynthia called from the back of the house.

"I have to go," the housekeeper whispered and shut the door.

Brenna drove back down Laurel Hill through the winding estates, wondering what she should do next. She was sure that the trunk in the photo was the same one that Ripley had bobbed to shore in, but if Cynthia hadn't owned it, then who had?

The trunk was the key. She needed to know where this picture had been taken. But it wasn't as if she could go knocking on every door in town, looking for a paneled room that was missing a trunk.

She turned a sharp corner on the hill, and all of Morse Point rolled out before her like a picnic blanket on a Sunday afternoon. This explained why the wealthy lived on Laurel Hill. The view of the small New England town was breathtaking. She could see the steeple of the Congregational Church on the green and the rim of the lake on the far side of town. Even old Mr. Cooper's barn was visible, perched in the middle of an empty farm field out past the elementary school.

She realized with a start that in the year she had lived here, she had learned a great deal about the town and its residents. She wondered if in forty years she'd be a walking town archive like the Porter sisters.

That was it. Brenna smacked her forehead. Why hadn't she thought of it before? The Porter sisters—they'd know where this photo was taken. She was sure of it.

Ten minutes later, she was back in the center of town and parked in front of the Porter sisters' cottage. A bungalow built in 1929, it sat on a residential street just off the center of town. Butter yellow with a white picket fence and green shutters, it was charming.

Brenna grabbed the manila folder that held the original photo of the Ripleys and hoped she found the sisters home. She pulled the chain of the captain's bell that hung by the front door and waited on the narrow porch.

The screen door swung wide and she stepped back as two gray heads popped out at her.

"I said I'd get it," Marie snapped.

"Well, I didn't hear you," Ella said.

"Yes, you did."

"No, I didn't."

"Hello, ladies," Brenna said, trying to break up the tiff. "Sorry to drop by without calling first."

"Not at all," Marie said. "Come in, come in."

"Yes, do," Ella said. "I was just finishing a batch of peanut butter cookies. I'll fetch you some."

"I made chocolate chip yesterday, if you'd rather," Marie offered.

Brenna followed them down a narrow hallway past the sitting room and dining room and into the kitchen. The house was bright and airy with hardwood floors and lots of windows. Pretty area rugs were scattered here and there. The walls were painted a soothing eggshell, and photos crowded every surface as if to keep a watchful eye on the bickering siblings.

The kitchen appeared to have had its last face-lift in the 1950s. The counters were small aqua tiles with white grout, and the gas oven was a vintage O'Keefe & Merritt.

An oval chrome table with matching aqua vinyl chairs sat in the center of the room and Ella gestured for Brenna to take a seat. The smell of peanut butter was thick in the air and she felt her stomach gurgle.

A plate of peanut butter cookies was plunked in front of her with an icy glass of milk. Brenna couldn't resist. The cookie was warm and melted in her mouth.

"Delicious," she said. Ella beamed. Marie frowned and shoved a plate of chocolate chip cookies in front of her as well. Brenna quickly took one and pronounced it delicious as well. Marie looked mollified, but Ella looked smug. Brenna shook her head. Sixty-plus years of sibling rivalry and still going strong.

"Now what can we do for you?" Marie asked. She took a seat at the table and helped herself to a cookie. She did not touch her sister's.

"Well, I have a picture from the inside of a house," Brenna said. She wasn't sure how much to tell them, so she hedged. "I believe it's a house here in Morse Point, but I can't be sure. As the unofficial town historians, I thought you two might recognize it."

They both preened under the flattery. Brenna had figured that might grease the wheels. She took out the full photo of Mayor Ripley and Cynthia. She didn't want to show them the enlargement and risk giving away the fact that she was tracking the owner of the trunk. She figured it might do the Porter sisters in to have to keep that information to themselves. She slid the picture toward them.

"Isn't this the photo you were having reduced to fit on the collage?" Ella asked.

"Yes," Brenna said. "Do you recognize where it was taken?"

"Why do you need to know?" Marie asked. She was leaning against her sister, trying to get as close to the photo as possible, and Ella was pushing back just as hard.

Brenna hoped they couldn't make out the vague form of the trunk behind the mayor.

"Oh, I just wanted to gather some background on each of the photos," she said. "To figure out how to lay them out, you know, by importance."

It was a complete bald-faced, bare-butted lie, but she maintained eye contact without blinking, and both sisters nodded.

"Let's see," Ella said. "Not much to go on here."

"That's Cynthia's blue number," Marie said. "She favored that gown for the big events."

"Like the governor's ball," Ella said.

"So, this isn't local?" Brenna asked, feeling a sharp jab of disappointment.

"I couldn't say," Ella said with a sniff. "I've never been to the governor's ball."

"I have," Marie trilled. "But I don't recognize it as part of the mansion."

"How could you recognize it?" Ella ground out. "It's not as if you got to see every room in the mansion. You only went to one event there and that's because you stole my date."

"I did not," Marie snapped.

"Did too," Ella barked. "John Henry thought he was asking me out, and you let him think you were me."

"I did not."

Brenna's head whipped back and forth between them. It was like watching a geriatric Ping-Pong match. She had a feeling this could go on all day. She didn't have all day.

"Ladies, were there any other events that Cynthia wore this gown to?" she asked.

"The harvest ball," Marie said. "I remember it distinctly because you took my rose-colored shawl."

"I borrowed it," Ella said.

"Borrowing means you ask first," Marie snapped.

"Like you should have when you took John Henry," Ella bit back.

Brenna sighed. She could feel a tic start in her right eye.

"Ladies, where was the harvest ball held?" she shouted over them.

They both blinked at her as if to say "duh."

"The Portsmyth mansion, of course," they said.

"The Portsmyths host it every November," Marie said.

"It's the social event of the season," Ella added.

And just like that, it all made sense.

"Thank you," Brenna said. "Thank you both!"

She jumped up from the table and raced back down the narrow hall to the door.

"What do you suppose that was about?" Ella asked her sister as they watched the door bang shut behind Brenna.

"Not a clue," Marie answered with a shake of her head.

"She's a nice girl, but a bit of busybody, don't you think?"

"Absolutely," Marie agreed. "I think all that city living must make for a certain amount of nosiness."

"Good thing we're more cultured than that," Ella said.

"Quite right, Sister, quite right," Marie said. "We'll just have to take her under our wing."

In unison they each took one of their cookies and dunked it into their milk, nibbling the edges and working their way around its circumference like synchronized swimmers.

# Chapter 22

Use fine-grain sandpaper in between coats of polyure-
thane and wipe clean with a sponge before coating again.

Brenna parked in front of Vintage Papers, barely remember-
ing to lock the Jeep in her haste. She hurtled through the
front door. She had to talk to Tenley before she made her
next move.

She found her friend working the counter, ringing up a
purchase for Susanna Blair. Susanna's daughter was having her sweet sixteen birthday party next month, and she
had custom-ordered the invitations from them weeks ago.
They were lovely, sporting glittery pink 16s in a retro font
on a cream-colored background.

Both women turned to stare at her as she banged into
the shop, and Brenna knew she must look like a crazy
person. If they knew the half of it! She smoothed her hair
with her hands and forced herself to breathe. The transaction seemed to take forever as Susanna described the cake,
DJ, and party favors in great glorious detail. Just when

Brenna didn't think she could stand another word, Susanna took her package and left.

"I need to ask you a question," she said as soon as the front door closed.

"Well, hello to you, too," Tenley said. "Fire away."

Brenna pulled out the envelope of pictures she'd gotten from the copy store and went to the back table.

She spread out the smaller ones to be used on the plaque and left the enlargement in the envelope.

Tenley followed her and asked, "What's up?"

"If I killed someone, would you help me dispose of the body?" Brenna asked.

"Why? Has someone been annoying you lately?" she asked.

"Hypothetically, I mean," Brenna said. "I'm asking as your best friend, would you help me?"

"I don't know." Tenley pondered the question. "Do I like the person?"

"Hmm, good question," she said. She chewed her lower lip. Did Phyllis like Mayor Ripley? As an outsider, it was hard for her to say. "Let's say you don't have any feelings one way or another."

"I don't know," Tenley said. "I suppose I would probably decide in the heat of the moment."

Brenna nodded. That made sense. It was hard to know what you'd do until the situation arose.

"What's going on, Brenna?" she asked.

"I think Cynthia murdered the mayor and I think Phyllis helped her dispose of the body," she said.

Tenley sat down hard on one of the chairs at the table. Her mouth was opening and closing in shock. Brenna took out the enlarged picture and told her about the trunk being Phyllis's and how Grace had overheard the mayor and Mrs. Ripley having a nasty fight the day of his murder.

"That doesn't prove that Cynthia killed him," Tenley said. "Or that Phyllis helped."

"Not yet it doesn't," Brenna said.

"What are you thinking?" Tenley asked.

"That Ed might have been on to something and that's why he got smacked on the head," she said. "I'm going to go to the hospital and see if he's awake. Maybe he remembers something."

"I'll come with you," Tenley offered.

"No, I need you to call Nate and tell him what's going on," Brenna said.

Tenley studied her. "Is there a reason you're not calling Nate?"

"No," Brenna said.

She knew her voice sounded falsely light, but it couldn't be helped. After telling Nate she wouldn't get involved, she did not want to be the one to call him and tell him just how involved she was. It was cowardly, she supposed, but he wouldn't get mad at Tenley. And once he had time to process the news, she was sure he wouldn't be mad at her either.

Tenley didn't believe her—Brenna could tell by the way she was frowning at her—but no matter. Brenna had bigger things on her to-do list, like catch a killer.


The elderly woman at the volunteer desk in the hospital lobby told Brenna to follow the yellow line through the swinging doors, to the elevators, up to Floor 3, and resume following the yellow line to Room 317, where she would find Ed.

Brenna managed it without getting lost, for which she was quite proud of herself. The hospital was cold and smelled of antiseptic and other more noxious things, like certain bodily fluids, that she didn't want to think about. She rounded the nurses' station and stopped short. Standing in front of Ed's room, arguing with a uniformed security guard, was Dom Cappicola.

Brenna watched the exchange. It did not appear to be going in Dom's favor. Finally, he thrust a handful of balloons at the guard and stalked away, heading straight for Brenna.

He looked up and their gazes locked. She was struck again by the powerful aura he seemed to wear like an overcoat. She was surprised the security guard had had the wherewithal to refuse him entry. She got the distinct impression that Dom Cappicola generally got what he went after.

"Brenna," he said. "It's good to see you."

"You, too," she said. She held out her hand, which he looked at in amusement. Before she had a chance to back up, he leaned in and kissed her cheek instead. She got a subtle scent of masculine aftershave that made her senses buzz and she stepped back quickly.

"I take it you came to see Ed," she said.

"Yeah, I heard about what happened, and I didn't want him worried that we'd shut the paper down while he was flat on his back," he said.

"You'll wait until he's upright?" she teased.

"Big of me, isn't it?" he asked with a self-deprecating grin.

Brenna smiled. She couldn't help it. Dom Cappicola had charm; she had to give him that.

"Unfortunately, the monkey with the plastic badge

won't let me in," Dom said. He threw a glance toward the officer in front of Ed's door, and his eyes narrowed in speculation.

Brenna followed his gaze. She mirrored his frown when she spotted Phyllis Portsmyth coming down the opposite hallway to stop in front of Ed's door.

"I am going to be seriously annoyed if they let the mayor's wife in when they wouldn't let me in to see my own employee," he said.

They watched silently as Phyllis was turned away. She glared at the officer and looked as if she wanted to kick him with the pointy toe of one of her shoes. Instead, she trudged back the way she came.

"Well, I guess political clout isn't what it used to be," Dom said. He looked somewhat mollified.

"Maybe, but that wasn't the mayor's wife," Brenna said.

"Sure it was," he said.

"No," Brenna said. "I just saw the mayor's wife, Cynthia, at their house. That is Phyllis Portsmyth, socialite extraordinaire."

"Well, isn't that interesting?" Dom asked. He rubbed his chin with the back of his hand.

"How so?" she asked.

"Because that woman, Phyllis, is the woman Ripley had with him when he came down to Bayview to talk business," he said. "And if she's not his wife . . ."

He let his sentence dangle and Brenna felt it ripple through her like a shock wave.

"Are you absolutely sure?" she asked.

Dom looked affronted. "Of course I'm sure. She reeks of old money and good breeding, which is why I assumed she was his wife. Not to mention that yellow rock on her hand is the size of a Buick—hard to forget a thing like that."

Brenna knew the ring he meant as she'd stared at it plenty of times herself. Phyllis wore the yellow Portsmyth diamond everywhere; it was five carats of hard-to-forget, in-your-face conspicuous consumption. This changed everything!

"Dom, you're brilliant!"

Impulsively, she grabbed his face and kissed him hard. When she would have stepped away, he caught her waist, met her gaze, and kissed her back. The contact was electric, like jamming a fork in an outlet but in a good way. She hadn't seen that coming.

When he released her, he took in her expression with a grin of satisfaction and a lingering look, which swept her from head to toe. Brenna got the feeling she amused him, but it wasn't just amusement in his eyes now. There was also desire. Brenna swallowed hard. She was not ready to process this.

"I've got to go," she said. With an awkward wave, she ran down the hall on legs that felt as sturdy as jelly.

# Chapter 23

If the sealant ever chips, sand it and protect it with another coat to preserve the piece.

Brenna left the hospital with her heart hammering in her throat, and not just because of Dom, although that didn't help.

No, this was it. Now she had a motive for the mayor's murder. Cynthia must have murdered her husband when she found out he was sleeping with her best friend.

It was a twenty-minute drive back to the center of town. Brenna spent it wondering what she should do next. She could go to Chief Barker, but what could she say, that Cynthia was the murderer? And what about the trunk? How did the mayor get in Phyllis's trunk?

The way Brenna had it figured, Cynthia found out about the affair and murdered her husband in a fit of rage. She then must have blackmailed Phyllis, by threatening to go public with the affair, into helping her dispose of the body in her steamer trunk. Obviously, the two women were in it together, which made sense since they were each other's alibi, but right now it was Brenna's word against theirs, unless she could get her hands on the murder weapon. But what was it?

The chief said that Ripley had sustained a head trauma and they'd searched Nate's house looking for evidence to that effect, but with no success. Cynthia must have hit him with something, and Brenna was pretty sure the police would have searched her house, too. Maybe she had hidden it with Phyllis or . . .

Brenna slammed on the brakes, causing the Jeep to teeter and lurch. Luckily, no one else was on this stretch of road or she would have caused a pile-up for sure. She couldn't believe it. All this time the murder weapon had been sitting on a shelf at Vintage Papers, and Brenna had never suspected. How could she have been so stupid?

She stomped on the gas. She had to get back to the shop and fast.

She called Chief Barker first, but he was out so she left a message. Then she called Nate. All awkwardness aside, this did concern him as he was still regarded as suspect number one. He didn't answer his phone either, and she sincerely hoped he hadn't been dragged in for questioning again or, even worse, arrested.

She parked down the street from the shop and hurried up the walk. She pulled on the front door but it was locked. Odd. She fished out her keys and let herself in.

"Tenley?" she called.

She made a beeline for the birdhouse sitting on the shelf. She'd take it over to Chief Barker and tell him her theory. The worst he could do would be to laugh her out of the office. The best he could do would be to deliver it to the crime lab and check for traces of Mayor Ripley's blood.

She stopped in front of the shelf. An empty cavity was all that remained of where the birdhouse used to sit. She glanced on the other shelves to see if it had been moved.

"Looking for this?"

Brenna spun around to find Phyllis standing behind her holding the birdhouse.

"An unlikely murder weapon, don't you think?"

"I'm not sure what you mean," Brenna said. Her scalp prickled as if it had been pulled taut.

"Sure you do." Phyllis's laugh was brittle. "Cynthia bashed her husband's skull in with this very birdhouse."

There was a manic light in Phyllis's eyes that reminded Brenna of a rabid dog, and she felt an overwhelming wave of fear infuse her body with a terrified paralysis. She was afraid to move lest Phyllis attack, and yet every cell in her body seemed to be leaning toward the door, so she slowly put one foot behind her and began to walk in that direction.

"Oh, don't leave." Phyllis's voice was soft, but the warning was unmistakable. "I've been waiting for you. I saw you, you know, kissing Dom Cappicola at the hospital. I hope it was worth it."

"Meaning?" Brenna asked.

"I know he saw me in Bayview as I'm sure he told you," Phyllis said.

She stepped aside and Brenna saw Tenley and Cynthia sitting tied up at the workroom table behind her. Their wrists and ankles were bound and a wide swath of silver tape covered their mouths. Brenna felt a hard punch of dread sock her in the middle, and she about doubled up. She had been wrong. So wrong.

"Phyllis, what are you doing?" she asked. "Let them go."

"No, I don't think so," Phyllis said.

She put the birdhouse down and fished a shiny silver lighter out of her Coach clutch. She picked up one of the photos of Ripley that Brenna had left on the table. She held the corner delicately between two manicured fingers while she ignited the opposite corner with the lighter.

Brenna felt her mouth go dry as the image of Ripley curled and charred under the hungry flame. The smell of smoke burnt her nose and she watched as Phyllis dropped the photo just before it reached her fingertips, letting the ashen remnants float to the floor.

"I think this shop will make a nice bonfire. Paper burns so well, you know," Phyllis said.

Brenna turned to run for help, but Phyllis dropped the lighter and grabbed an X-Acto Knife.

"Stop!" she ordered as she stepped back and pressed the blade against Tenley's throat. "One more step and I'll slit her throat."

Brenna froze.

"Sit," Phyllis said. She gestured to an empty seat opposite Tenley. She rolled the duct tape to Brenna and told her to tape her ankles together. Seeing no alternative, Brenna complied.

Phyllis kept the knife at Tenley's throat while she used her free hand to tape Brenna's wrists together. Brenna would have fought her off but she was afraid Tenley would get hurt, a fact she knew Phyllis was counting on. The three of them sat facing one another while Phyllis hurriedly locked the front door again.

Tenley and Cynthia were both wide-eyed with shock. Brenna knew she must appear the same. It wasn't a good look.

Phyllis returned and pulled the tape off their mouths

with a rip. Tenley gasped for breath while Cynthia spat and coughed.

"Phyllis, why are you doing this?" Cynthia pleaded. She looked like a puppy shut out in the rain. "I thought we were friends."

Phyllis slapped her hard. Cynthia's head snapped back and a trickle of blood, where Phyllis's ring had cut her lip, ran down her chin.

"Don't call me that!" Phyllis said. She stabbed the table top with the X-Acto Knife as if she wished it were Cynthia's heart. She left the knife in the wood and leaned forward to stare at Cynthia with loathing. "Look at you. Do you really believe I considered you my friend?"

Cynthia cowered and Brenna felt bad for her.

"You, the girl who dragged herself out of the projects in Dorchester, be my friend? My family can trace its roots back to the *Mayflower*. You didn't deserve to be married to the mayor. That position of prominence should have been mine. You stole it from me."

"What?" Cynthia looked bewildered. "How?"

"When my husband died, the invitations stopped," Phyllis said, bitterness twisting her mouth into a sneer. "Suddenly, you were the social queen of Morse Point. You, Cynthia Ripley. Ha! I have the breeding and the class. You are nothing, not even worthy to clean my shoes."

Cynthia's face lost all its color. "It was you."

Phyllis threw back her head and let loose a shrill laugh that was chilling in its lack of humor. "Caught on, have you?"

"Y—you were the one having an affair with Jim," Cynthia said.

"What?" Tenley gasped.

"Oh, don't sound so shocked, Little Miss Morse Point. It's no worse than you slumming with your bartender, what's his name, Tom Collins? No, that's a drink. I bet he knows how to make a good one, though, doesn't he?" Phyllis purred.

Tenley hissed.

Cynthia seemed bewildered. "How long did it go on?"

"A little over a year," Phyllis said. "What can I say? He felt he needed someone more his social equal."

This was good, Brenna thought, they needed to keep her talking.

"Then why have an affair?" Brenna asked. "Why didn't he just leave Cynthia for you?"

"Perhaps you should ask his killer," Phyllis said as she circled Cynthia's chair.

"I didn't kill him," Cynthia protested. "When I left him, he was alive."

"Liar!" Phyllis yelled. "You bashed him on the head with that birdhouse. You wanted him dead."

"No, we had a fight. I was angry when I discovered he was cheating, but I never meant to kill him," she argued.

"But you left him," Phyllis said, continuing to circle like a vulture eyeing a carcass. "You left him there, bleeding on the floor. So, he came to me."

"I had to get away," Cynthia said. "I couldn't think. He was yelling at me after I hit him and I was afraid."

"Likely story," Phyllis scoffed. "When I found him—"

"When you found him?" Brenna interrupted. "I thought you said he came to you?"

"Don't interrupt me!" Phyllis screeched and raised her hand as if she'd hit her.

Brenna didn't flinch. If Phyllis came within striking distance, she planned to kick out her bound ankles and knock Phyllis down. As if sensing danger, Phyllis lowered her arm and backed up. She smirked at Brenna as if she knew what she was thinking.

"Fine then," she said. "I happened to be waiting outside. When Cynthia stormed out, I took Jim to my house for a little TLC."

Phyllis paced around the table until she stood behind Cynthia, who was now silently crying.

"That's right. I was going to take your husband." She ran a hand over Cynthia's short-cropped blond hair, a mimic of her own. "Just because you dress like me and talk like me, doesn't mean you can be me, you know. Jim knew the difference. He knew quality when he saw it."

Two red spots flared on Cynthia's cheeks.

"Really?" she snapped. "Then why did you kill him? Could it be because he wouldn't leave me for you?"

Phyllis sucked in a gasp of air through her teeth. "I didn't kill him."

"I don't believe you," Cynthia said. She glared at her former friend, looking stronger than she had in days. "When I left him, he was angry and bleeding but alive. You said you took him to your place, so what happened, Phyllis? What did you do to my husband?"

Phyllis paled. Her lips were pressed tightly together as if she hadn't anticipated Cynthia putting up a fight, and now she wasn't sure what to do.

"I think I can answer that," Brenna said, drawing their attention to her. "Phyllis stuffed Jim into the trunk in her study and then floated him in the lake, hoping no doubt that everyone would think Nate did it."

"How did you . . . what makes you think . . . well, that's just . . ." Phyllis's voice trailed off.

"I found Jim in the trunk," Brenna said. "I got a pretty

good look at it. Cynthia gave me a picture from the Harvest Ball, taken in your study in front of the same trunk. I recognized it."

"Where is it? Where's the photo?" Phyllis snapped.

"I gave it to Chief Barker," Brenna lied. "He'll be here any minute."

Phyllis's eyes grew wide and then narrowed. "Nice try."

Brenna shrugged. "What I can't figure out is why. Why'd you kill him, Phyllis?"

"Because," she spat. "While I was struggling to keep him conscious, he told me he could never leave dear Cynthia, because it would damage him politically. The bastard!"

Brenna looked past Phylis and saw Tenley leaning forward against the table. Her face was tight, and beads of sweat were popping out on her forehead. She was inching her hands across the table, trying to remove the X-Acto Knife with the tips of her fingers and not be noticed.

"So, you must have known Cynthia would be the primary suspect," Brenna said. She knew she had to keep her talking until Tenley could get the knife. "Why did you give Cynthia an alibi? Why didn't you let her take the fall? Wouldn't that have been the ultimate revenge?"

"It would have been, but don't you see?" Phyllis asked. "It was brilliant. When Jim's body was found in that trunk, Cynthia came to me and asked me to lie for her."

Cynthia nodded. "It's true," she said. "I knew that, as his wife, I'd be the prime suspect, and I had no alibi as I'd just been driving around, fuming about his affair."

"So when Cynthia asked me to lie for her, it was perfect," Phyllis said. "I lie for her and keep her forever in my debt. Meanwhile I save myself."

Brenna saw Tenley lower the knife to the floor. Her hands were bound more tightly than Brenna's. There was no way she could cut herself free. Out of the corner of her eye, she saw Tenley push the knife toward her with the toe of her sneaker. Brenna feigned a sneeze, and when Phyllis turned away in disgust, she bent and swiftly grabbed the handle of the blade. Working under the cover of the table top, she wedged the handle between her knees and quietly worked the tape across the blade, while Tenley distracted Phyllis.

"I don't believe you," Tenley said. "There's no way you could have stuffed the mayor into a trunk and shoved him into the lake all by yourself. You're too old."

Phyllis's eyes widened with outrage. She lifted her left arm and made a muscle, which she patted with her free hand.

"I'll have you know, I'm in excellent physical condition," Phyllis said. "Jim could tell you. I held a pillow over his face until he was gone. Then I hefted him into the trunk. The pillow was the hardest part, as he put up a bit of a fuss. But then I used a dolly and my gardener's pickup truck to load the trunk and drive it to the lake. No one can tie me to the crime. In fact, the one person who saw the truck thought it was Nate Williams's truck."

Phyllis was facing Cynthia, as if enjoying telling her the grisly details of her husband's death. Brenna took the opportunity to slash through the tape on Tenley's wrists and then passed the knife to Tenley so she could free Cynthia.

"So, why did you go after Ed?" Brenna asked. "He was helping you out by printing stories that Nate was the murderer."

"That little weasel," Phyllis scoffed. "He wouldn't let

it go. He questioned the witness who saw the truck and they got a partial license plate that did not match Nate Williams's plate. When he came to talk to Patrick, I knew he'd figured out it was Patrick's truck and not Nate's."

Brenna remembered Ed had said, "The plate doesn't match," when they found him in the alley. He'd been talking about the license plates. It all seemed so obvious now.

"He wasn't supposed to live, and once I'm done here, I don't imagine he will for much longer," Phyllis said.

Brenna felt a chill go up her spine. Phyllis wasn't just a rebuffed lover, who had gotten carried away when she went for revenge; she was straight-up crazy.

Just then, Cynthia erupted from the table with a guttural roar. Phyllis grabbed another knife from a nearby shelf and tried to fend her off, but Cynthia was a force of fury. She slapped the knife out of Phyllis's hand and with claws out, she went right for her eyes. Phyllis tucked her head and covered up with her arms, but Cynthia just switched direction and went for her hair. Growing up in the projects in Boston had given Cynthia some skills.

"What's the matter, Phyllis?" Cynthia taunted her. "You can't subdue me by threatening to hurt Tenley now, can you?"

Phyllis shrieked. Brenna and Tenley exchanged glances as they jumped from their seats. The two women were crab-walking across the room, spinning as Phyllis tried to wriggle out of Cynthia's hold. Meanwhile, Cynthia was using her free hand to slap or punch any part of Phyllis she could reach.

"Call the police," Brenna ordered, and Tenley raced for the phone.

"You lying—cheating—murdering—" Cynthia punctu-

ated each word with a hit. The last few words were buried
as she bent over to get a better grip on Phyllis.

Phyllis shimmied out of her hold, dropped to the floor,
and then dashed for the door. Brenna went to step in front
of her, but Phyllis raised her hand and Brenna saw the
glint of the X-Acto Knife. She ducked and rolled out of
the way.

Cynthia was not about to let her get away, however.
Just before Phyllis reached the door, Cynthia launched
herself at the other woman in a move reminiscent of an
NFL defensive tackle. They hit the glass door with such
force that they shattered it, the momentum carrying them
through the shards to the street beyond.

Brenna ran through the gaping hole and saw Cynthia,
sitting on top of Phyllis, and despite the fact that she was
scratched and bleeding, Cynthia wore a look of triumph
while she held the X-Acto-Knife in one hand and a chunk
of Phyllis's hair in the other.

Tenley appeared at Brenna's elbow.

"Chief Barker is on his way," she said.

In the distance, Brenna could hear a siren wail. Heads
poked out of the shops surrounding them as people started
to gather and stare.

Phyllis was wailing almost louder than the chief's car
when he pulled up, but Cynthia ignored her.

"Quit whining," she snapped, and she sat down harder
on Phyllis's lower back.

Matt ran down the sidewalk, pushing past the gawkers,
to get to Tenley. Without pausing, he grabbed her and
hugged her close.

"Are you all right?" he asked. "I heard the crash from
the restaurant."

"Fine," she said. It was a blatant lie. Her hands were shaking as she shoved a stray lock of blond hair behind her ear. Matt looped an arm around her, locking her to his side.

"Brenna!" a voice called, and she glanced up to see Nate pushing his way through the crowd to get to her.

An arm draped around her from the right, however, and she turned to find Dom Cappicola standing beside her.

"Are you okay?" he asked. "I heard the commotion all the way at Stan's."

"I'm fine," she said. It felt good to have something solid to lean against, and she took a moment to appreciate his warmth and his strength.

When she looked up, Nate was in front of them, glaring at Dom as if he'd stolen his parking spot.

Chief Barker hauled Cynthia off Phyllis. Both women started screeching at the same time, and Phyllis took a swing at Cynthia. Chief Barker seemed to decide they both needed to be subdued. So, Phyllis was handcuffed and put in the chief's car, while Cynthia was handcuffed and put in Officer DeFalco's car.

"Brenna Miller." The chief barked her name and she jumped, stepping away from Dom and Nate. He seemed at a loss for words. "Explain."

She did. It was the short version, but he got the gist.

"Can you and Tenley come over to the station and give statements?" he asked her.

"Sure." She nodded.

"I'll give you a lift," Dom offered.

"No, I'll take her," Nate said.

The two men stared at one another for a second. Ridiculous.

"I think I'll just walk," Brenna said. She strode through

the crowd and back into the paper store to get her purse. Tenley, looking flushed, met her in the storeroom.

"What happened here? How did Phyllis tie you two up?" Brenna asked the question that had been bothering her since she'd found them bound and gagged.

Tenley looked pained. "Phyllis snuck up behind me, and before I knew it I was duct taped like a leaky pipe. Then Cynthia came in, and Phyllis threatened to cut me if Cynthia didn't tape herself up, much like she did with you."

"I never suspected Phyllis," Brenna said.

"Me neither," Tenley agreed. "Quite a day, eh?"

"I'll say."

"We'd better go. The Porter sisters are going to watch the shop while we're at the station."

"Good," Brenna said. She handed Tenley her purse and grabbed her own. As they made their way to the door, Tenley gave her a funny look.

"What? Is there glass in my hair?" Brenna asked.

"No, but Dom and Nate look ready to club one another out there, and Ruby Wolcott said that a nurse at the hospital, Kim Lebrowski, confirmed what Phyllis said about you kissing Dom right in the middle of the critical care unit," Tenley said. "Is this true?"

Brenna groaned. "Yes."

"I thought you liked Nate," she said.

"I do," Brenna said. "But . . . it's complicated."

"And Dom?" she asked.

"He's just . . ." Brenna trailed off and Tenley said, "Hot."

"Yeah," Brenna agreed. "I like them both. Is that bad?"

"Not if you don't mind having an admirer or two." Tenley tried not to laugh and failed miserably.

"Maybe I'll get lucky and Chief Barker will arrest me," Brenna said.

"You can always hope."

They pushed their way through the crowd, ignoring the murmurs that followed them, and strode down the sidewalk to the police station on the corner with their heads held high.

Brenna sat on her front steps, watching the amber rays of the setting sun reflected in the glassy surface of the lake. She had a batch of brownies in the oven, and the scent of baking chocolate wafted on the air in tantalizing bursts.

A bark sounded and she looked up to see Hank bounding toward her. His golden hair looked aflame in the setting sun, and she grinned when he stopped in front of her and pressed his head against her leg, demanding love.

"Hiya, boy," she said. She hugged him close and buried her nose in his neck.

"Do I smell brownies?"

Brenna glanced up to see Nate striding down the path toward her. She felt her insides flip-flop at the sight of him. She hadn't been alone with him since the scene in front of the paper store. Even at the mayor's funeral, she had been sure to keep Tenley and Matt with her at all times, mostly to ward off the gossips, but also to avoid the awkwardness of talking to Nate. Now it seemed she had no choice.

"Don't tell me you could smell those brownies all the way over at your house?" she asked.

"I am downwind of your oven," he said. "It makes it very difficult to resist temptation."

He sat on the steps beside her. He wore his usual jeans

and a long-sleeved Henley. His thick brown hair was mussed, but his gray eyes were as intent as ever, and they swept over her as if doing inventory.

"You look better," he said.

She raised her eyebrows at him.

"As if you've gotten some rest," he clarified.

She nodded. She had, in fact, slept for fourteen hours.

"I wanted to thank you," Nate said. He turned his head and glanced out at the lake. As Brenna studied his profile, he seemed to be considering his words.

"When Ed dug up my past, I felt most people turn away from me," he said. "But not you."

"I am an excellent judge of character," Brenna said, hoping to lighten the somber tone. "I didn't believe all of those crazy articles about wild parties and trashed hotel rooms."

"You should have," Nate said. His voice was full of self-recrimination. "I left New York because I was becoming a person I didn't like. It wasn't as bad as Ed's story painted it, but I was a self-obsessed, self-indulgent jackass. I did berate the people unfortunate enough to be the ones looking after me. I began to loathe myself, the art world, all of it. I came here to find myself."

They were quiet for a moment. Brenna knew exactly how he felt. She had left Boston for a similar reason. She had felt herself becoming someone she didn't like, and she'd had to leave to find herself again.

"So have you succeeded?" she asked. "In finding yourself?"

"I think I found something better," he said. He took her hand in his and interlaced their fingers.

Brenna felt her pulse do a skip-to-my-Lou. Okay. What did he mean and how could she ask him?

The buzzer for the brownies went off, sending Hank into a frenzy of barking. A cabin door popped open across the lake, and Twyla stepped out.

"Do I smell brownies?" she called.

Brenna gently pulled her hand out of Nate's as she rose to her feet.

"Yep!" she called back.

"I've got vanilla ice cream. I'll be right over!"

Two more cabin doors popped open, and Portia and Paul joined Twyla in her trek around the lake.

"Nice to have everything back to the way it was, isn't it?" she asked.

His gray eyes shone silver in the coming twilight as he studied her.

"I don't think anything is ever going to be the same again, do you?" he asked.

The oven buzzer went off again, jolting Brenna out of her daze, and she hurried inside to save her brownies before they were burned beyond recognition. And that was exactly what she was afraid of if she got tangled up with Nate or Dom. That she wouldn't be smart enough to pull her pan out of the oven before she got burned.

Before the murder was solved, she had thought she might have to leave Morse Point for her peace of mind. But now that Phyllis was behind bars, she had no reason to leave. This was a town where nothing noteworthy had happened for fifty years. She found great comfort in that, and now she could stay, knowing that the only thing at risk was her heart. And after solving a murder, surely she could handle that.